"Be w...
"I d...... ...."

Mac's brows rose. "Sit next to a man?"

"Come running when a man whistles."

"What *do* you normally do?" His voice was lazy.

"Ignore him. The fact that I came at a dead run is just an indication of how desperate I am."

The lines at the corners of his eyes deepened. "For me?"

"Dream on." In a voice as brisk and cheery as she could make it, she clarified her statement. "Desperate to be rescued."

Heather leaned back, drew a deep breath and hoped that he couldn't see her face. She had never developed the art of concealing either her thoughts or her emotions, and right now she badly wanted to disguise both. Because whether it was his lazy smile, the look of masculine appreciation that gleamed in his green eyes, or simply everything falling into place, it was at that moment she realized that Wade Mackenzie was a dangerous man.

And she was a very susceptible woman.

Dear Reader:

1990 is in full swing, and so is Silhouette Romances' tenth anniversary celebration—the DIAMOND JUBILEE! To symbolize the timelessness of love, as well as the modern gift of the tenth anniversary, we're presenting readers with a DIAMOND JUBILEE Silhouette Romance title each month, penned by one of your favorite Romance authors.

This month, visit the American West with Rita Rainville's *Never on Sundae*, a delightful tale sure to put a smile on your lips. Losing weight is never so romantic as when Wade Mackenzie is around. He has lovely Heather Brandon literally pining away! Then, in April, Peggy Webb has written a special treat for readers—*Harvey's Missing*. Be sure not to miss this heartwarming romp about a man, a woman and a lovable dog named Harvey!

Victoria Glenn, Annette Broadrick, Dixie Browning, Lucy Gordon, Phyllis Halldorson—to name just a few—have written DIAMOND JUBILEE titles especially for you.

And that's not all! This month we have a very special surprise! Ten years ago, Diana Palmer published her very first romance. Now, some of them are available again in a three-book collection entitled Diana Palmer Duets. Each book will have two wonderful stories plus an introduction by the author. Don't miss them!

The DIAMOND JUBILEE Celebration, plus special goodies like Diana Palmer Duets, is Silhouette Books' way of saying thanks to you, our readers. We've been together for ten years now, and with the support you've given to us, you can look forward to many more years of heartwarming, poignant love stories.

I hope you'll enjoy this book and all of the stories to come. Come home to romance—Silhouette Romance—for always!

Sincerely,

Tara Hughes Gavin
Senior Editor

RITA RAINVILLE

Never
on Sundae

Silhouette Romance

Published by Silhouette Books New York

America's Publisher of Contemporary Romance

To Pat Teal

Agent extraordinaire, dear friend,
and a true connoisseur of chocolate!

SILHOUETTE BOOKS
300 E. 42nd St., New York, N.Y. 10017

ISBN: 0-373-08706-3

First Silhouette Books printing March 1990

Printed in the U.S.A.

Books by Rita Rainville

Silhouette Romance

Challenge the Devil #313
McCade's Woman #346
Lady Moonlight #370
Written on the Wind #400
The Perfect Touch #418
The Glorious Quest #448
Family Affair #478
It Takes a Thief #502
Gentle Persuasion #535
Never Love a Cowboy #556
Valley of Rainbows #598
No Way to Treat a Lady #663
Never on Sundae #706

Silhouette Desire

A Touch of Class #495

RITA RAINVILLE

has been a favorite with romance readers since the publication of her first book, *Challenge the Devil*, in 1984. More recently, she won the Romance Writers of America Golden Medallion Award for *It Takes a Thief*. She was also a part of the Silhouette Romance Homecoming Celebration as one of the authors featured in the "Month of Continuing Stars."

Rita has always been in love with books, especially romances. In fact, because reading has always been such an important part of her life, she has become a literacy volunteer and now teaches reading to those who have yet to discover the pleasure of a good book.

Southern California is home to this prolific and happily married author, who plans to continue writing romances for a long time to come.

A Note From The Author:

Dear Reader,

For more years than I care to remember, I dreamed of writing. And every now and then, sandwiched in between working outside of our home, raising two sons, keeping the homefires burning and attending evening college classes, I actually did write. A little.

And then in June of 1982, my husband, who was also doing all of the above, convinced me that the world wouldn't reel off its axis if I stayed home. To write. My time had come, he told me.

How did I react?

I was excited. And apprehensive. No, actually what I was was terrified. What if I *couldn't* write? What if I didn't have whatever it took to be a writer?

Ta-da! In November of 1983 I sold my first two books; this is now my fourteenth book for Silhouette.

The wonderful thing about dreams is that quite often they exceed your expectations. Not only am I writing and selling, I am also hearing from warm, wonderful people who *read* what I write. Thank you for your letters. You don't know how much they mean to me. I wish for you the same joy, so whatever it is that you want from life, *dare to dream*!

Sincerely,

Rita Rainville

Prologue

They're either going to have to wire my jaws shut or take me out and dump me in the desert!''

Succinctly put, Heather Brandon reflected, agreeing with the sentiment if not the drastic statement. Glancing down at the digital numbers between the handlebars, she pumped harder and waited for the reaction of the elderly woman on the Exercycle next to her. She wasn't disappointed. Maude Gunther's pudgy index finger prodded her in the ribs.

"Listen!" Maude hissed. "Isn't it exactly what I was saying? They're desperate!"

The two of them were sandwiched in the center of a long line of women who were pedaling with grim determination. The blonde several bikes down continued her lament.

"Even in the middle of the desert, surrounded by sagebrush and cactus needles, I probably wouldn't lose an ounce."

"Well, I'd like to give it a try," a brunette groaned, wiping a terry wristband over her sweaty brow. "If I didn't have to pass that frozen-yogurt place when I leave here, my life would be a lot easier."

"And the doughnut shop."

"For me, it's the deli."

"The pizza place."

"The croissant shop!"

As the plaintive comments rose above the whir of machines, Maude leaned closer to Heather. "I tell you, it'll work! All we have to do is fix up the place a bit."

"Umm." Heather gave an automatic nod and kept pedaling. She had heard it all before; a pit bull had nothing on her new friend when it came to tenacity.

What it boiled down to was that Maude had a huge piece of property somewhere between Phoenix and Tucson, with two old rambling houses set several hundred feet apart. She lived in one and she wanted Heather to help her turn the other one into a spa. It didn't have to be fancy, Maude had argued. It could be more like a homey retreat.

Maude nudged Heather again. "It can't miss," she insisted in a penetrating whisper. "You've heard them. At one time or another, they've all gone to those fancy places where they starve and torture people. If they pay good money for that, they'll do anything! And we can guarantee them a week that's free of temptation. They'll only be able to eat what we give them."

"Is your place really that far out in the sticks?"

Maude's nod was so vehement that a gray curl dipped down on her forehead. "Honey, you'd have to see it to believe it. And the best part is that they'd have to leave their cars behind, because only a four-wheel-drive can handle the last part of the road. They couldn't get out until we took them out, and that means they couldn't get to food. Do you realize what a favor we'd be doing them?"

Before Heather could answer, the blonde groaned.

"How many miles do I have to pedal to burn off a hot fudge sundae?"

"Your legs will fall off before that happens," her neighbor told her.

"Listen!" Maude hissed again. "I tell you, Heather, they're singing our song!"

Chapter One

You've turned Maude's ranch into a *fat farm*?"

Heather Brandon eyed the man towering over her and sighed in pure exasperation. She should be accustomed to unannounced visitors roaming through the house with raised brows, she thought, but the last thing she needed today was another cowboy grinning over the changes in the old house.

"Maude and I call it a retreat," she said in a deliberate, take-it-or-leave-it tone.

He left it. Shoving his large hands in the back pockets of his worn jeans, his narrowed gaze swept the room, stopped at the mirrored walls, then gave each of the four Exercycles a brief, thorough inspection. "This is the master bedroom," he told her.

It wasn't news to Heather. So far, every visitor had mentioned it. "*Was* the master bedroom."

Heather inched around him to set a luxuriant ivy plant on the corner table, her antennae quivering at the tone of his voice. There wasn't a trace of amusement in it, concealed or otherwise, she decided. And he definitely wasn't smiling.

"It's where people sleep," he informed her.

Turning the plant, she nodded cheerfully. "You're right, they did. Once."

"It's where *I* sleep."

"*Used* to," she murmured absentmindedly, stepping back and tilting her head to stare critically at the mirrored image of the leafy vine. Unfortunately, since the blond giant had planted himself right next to it, she also got a good look at him. If ever a man was dying for an argument, she decided with an inward sigh, it was this one.

While she examined eyes as green as the ivy and an expression as hard as his biceps, his words finally registered.

Sleep? Him? Here? Who the devil was he? Obviously not a potential patron. Even if they catered to men—which they didn't—there wasn't a thing they could offer him. Whatever he weighed, his large frame put every pound to good use. Very good use. Nor did he look like the type who would send his wife to them. But then, she concluded with a thoughtful blink, he didn't look like the type who *had* a wife. There was a certain untamed quality about him that shouted *single*. And prowling.

Deciding that the plant could take care of itself, Heather aimed a polite smile at over six feet of muscle and turned away. She didn't know where he'd come from and she didn't know what he wanted, but she had no doubt he'd manage just fine without her.

"Hold on a minute." A large, tanned hand with a dusting of gold hair settled gently on her shoulder. Without seeming to exert any pressure at all, it stopped her in her tracks. "I'll walk along with you."

"I'm only going to the next room," she replied absently, one part of her mind focusing on the warmth of that hand, another part on her missing friend. Where was Maude *this* time? Right from the beginning, when there had been a constant stream of neighbors and acquaintances dropping in to visit, the older woman had rarely been there to greet them. Last week it had been their poker-faced Navajo neighbor, Joe Eagle. Yesterday, it had been Mr. Gottschalk, a small, sinewy, bowlegged man who owned the next ranch, and the day before that, plump, apple-cheeked *Mrs*. Gottschalk and two of her neighbors. And now, a man the size of a mountain was about to follow her down the wide hall.

She wasn't nervous, Heather assured herself. Not exactly. People in this southern section of Arizona were friendly, but she *was* alone with him. The workmen had been gone for several days, the hands were all out doing whatever hands did on an early summer morning, and God only knew where Maude was.

It wasn't that she minded playing hostess, Heather told herself, stepping through the doorway, her nerve endings informing her that he was right behind her. She had met a number of interesting people in the three months that she'd been here, but right now she simply didn't have time to stop and entertain drop-ins.

Or to pump them for information. Most of them had at least offered their names before they'd moved from room to room and stared openmouthed at the changes in the old house. This one hadn't.

"I'll just follow along," he said, walking beside her. "Wherever you're going is fine with me."

His words didn't reassure her, nor did the promise in his deep voice. The last thing she needed was a larger-than-life shadow trailing her through the rambling house while she checked the linens, soap dishes, flowers and the myriad small touches involved in preparing for their first clients. But for Maude's sake, she wouldn't send him on his way—assuming, of course, that he could be dislodged with anything less than a stick of dynamite—because she'd learned in the past few months that Maude knew everyone for miles around, and whatever the time of day or night her friends were always welcome.

Heather stood in the doorway of the first bedroom taking in the spare, uncluttered look of the southwestern decor. Her fingers itched to fluff up the pillows on the bed, but she restrained herself, knowing it was tension rather than necessity that prodded her. In two days the house would be full of women . . . and right now she had a man standing behind her, emanating enough energy to light the city of Tucson.

She compromised by moving to the window and adjusting the creamy vertical blinds, noting absently that the sunlight slashing through the window wasn't nearly as warm as the body heat she'd just encountered. After reminding herself that while it was annoying that he hadn't introduced himself, silence still wasn't a crime, she turned back to face the watchful man.

Meeting his steady gaze, she held out her hand. "I'm Heather Brandon, Maude's . . . partner."

Instead of shaking her hand, he cradled it, tugging her a bit closer as he wrapped long fingers around her wrist, turning it, examining her palm as if he'd never seen one before.

"Partner?" Tawny brows raised another notch.

"Partner," she said firmly, tugging at her hand. Since Maude, by defection, had apparently turned the entire project over to her, she was entitled, she assured herself.

"Wade Mackenzie," he said finally, waiting.

Heather tilted her head, regarding him thoughtfully, then allowed herself a soft sigh. He obviously expected a reaction of some kind, so she mentally sifted through the conversations she'd had with Maude—and drew a blank. As far as she was concerned, Wade Mackenzie was just a name. It belonged to no rancher, no cowboy, no neighbor that she knew of. Nobody. But this man, she decided, slowly withdrawing her hand from his grasp, had more than mere size going for him. Everything from his scuffed boots to his watchful gaze proclaimed the fact. In an understated way, he was a power to contend with; he was definitely not a nobody.

"Known Maude for long?" she prodded delicately, shifting beneath his interested glance.

"Yeah, you might say that." He gazed around the room with the same lack of appreciation he'd demonstrated in the former master bedroom.

"Friend of the family?" She waited while he thumbed the brim of his hat back a notch and considered her question, his light eyes shifting back to her face in an unblinking assessment.

"I *am* the family," he said finally. "At least, part of it."

For the first time, Heather understood what people meant when they said their hearts dropped to their toes. She also, finally, made the connection. It was true that Maude hadn't mentioned Wade Mackenzie, but several times a day she had brought "Mac" into the conversation—her nephew, or cousin, or whatever he was. Her *difficult* relative Mac. No, Heather amended silently, to give him his due, she'd said he wasn't difficult about everything, just about a house. *This* house. If she had understood Maude correctly, he was a charming man with a pleasant disposition. But when he got his first glimpse of the transformation the house had undergone, Maude admitted, his even temper would probably level out at somewhere around nasty.

Taking another look at the man before her, Heather saw no reason to doubt a thing Maude had said—except the charming part. He lounged in the doorway, leaning one broad shoulder against the jamb, his bland gaze resembling that of a drowsy lion. Lazy as it was, she'd bet the chocolate-chip cookie she had saved for dessert that he had already drawn some major conclusions about her pantie and bra size, and was doing some heavy cogitating on the state of her love life.

"Did Maude know you were coming?" Heather squeezed by him and walked briskly down the hall to the next room. The thud of his boots on the tiled floor told her he was right behind her.

"Yep."

That figured she thought crossly. Maude—endearing, infuriating Maude—was as nosy as a friendly pup, always trotting ahead to see what was around the next bend, leaving the present to take care of itself. And Maude hated confrontations. Heather had learned early in the venture that if a snag occurred with the plumbing or painting, Maude would be conspicuous by her absence.

"She'll be sorry that she missed you." Heather opened the next door and walked in, stopping in the center of the Victorian room.

"I'll be around."

That was exactly what she was afraid of. His deep voice was slow and soft, full of promise, and she had a strong feeling that he was a man who kept his word. Automatically, she twitched the lace curtains and smoothed the puffy, flowered bedspread.

"I don't know when she'll be back."

"I'll wait."

She turned back to him. "It may be late."

"I've got plenty of time."

Well, *she* didn't. Just for starters, she had to check the rest of the bedrooms, remove a splash of paint from the tile in the small bathroom, and oil the new oak table in the sitting room—and she didn't want to do a single one of those things with him breathing down her neck. "I don't want to be rude, Mr. Mackenzie, but—"

"Mac."

"What?"

"My friends call me Mac."

"I hardly know you," she pointed out reasonably.

"You will."

"Mr. Macken—"

"Mac."

Mackenzie watched her take a steadying breath and toss him an aggravated look. And in that instant, he knew. It was that simple, that quick. He knew that Heather Brandon was going to be his.

"All right. *Mac!*"

He grinned. "What?"

"What do you mean, *what*?"

"You started to tell me something," he reminded her patiently, enjoying the frustration snapping in her brown eyes. The effort she made to gather her scattered thoughts would have been visible to a blind man.

"Oh. Well, it's just that I've—"

"Got a lot to do?"

"Uh, yes." She drew another breath. "And I don't—"

"Have time to entertain me?"

"Well . . . yes."

"And you want to get on with whatever it is that you have to do?"

She nodded, narrowing her eyes.

"And you don't want me in your hair while you're doing it?" Anticipation washed through him, watching her face as relief battled with civility. Civility won, he noted with amusement. Just barely.

"Of course," she said carefully, "you *are* used to visiting, and I wouldn't want to—"

"Good," he said briskly, moving aside and giving
her just enough room to step out into the hall. "Then
I'll just tag along with you and take a look at what
you've done to the old place." When her jaw dropped,
he raised a hand, palm facing her. "Look, I may not
like it, but that's my problem. I'll take care of myself.
Just pretend I'm not even here." Yeah, honey, you
just try. "I won't get in your way. I'll be fine." She
spun around and took off, the heels of her sandals
snapping a frustrated cadence on the tile flooring.
Yep, he decided, ambling behind the wrathful bundle
of femininity, he'd be just fine.

Even with exasperation straightening her spine like
a poker, Heather was worth watching. Her hair, a soft
brown with strands that gleamed gold and red in the
shafts of sunlight, was piled on top of her head in a
haphazard arrangement. It looked as soft as corn silk,
and only the conviction that she'd turn on him with
bared teeth kept him from touching the wisps that
were breaking loose and curling at her nape.

As for the rest of her... He pursed his lips in a
soundless whistle. She wasn't beautiful, but what she
had would do very nicely. Intelligence and humor
gleamed in those gorgeous brown eyes, and he'd bet
last month's paycheck that she had enough heat to
burn him to a cinder. As far as he was concerned—if
you disregarded the fact that she'd trashed his favorite house—she was perfect. Of course *she* most likely
wouldn't agree; there didn't seem to be a woman alive
who wasn't trying to trim inches away from one part
of her body and add them to another. But he *liked*
small, high breasts and a rounded bottom. And wide

eyes and soft lips. He lengthened his stride, keeping his eyes on the nice shape of her bottom. It was modestly covered by wheat-colored jeans and moved in the tantalizing sway that had tormented men since the beginning of time.

If he had any sense, he'd get out of here, he decided, his gaze sliding down the jeans to bare ankles and white, flimsy-looking sandals. It didn't take a genius to realize that Heather Brandon, cute rear and all, was turning the homestead upside down. A smart man would race back to Denver, he told himself. Then again, he mused, his gaze rising and halting at Heather's back pockets, a smart man was probably more cautious than he was. A smart man would never take one look at a woman and decide that he'd found what he'd spent a lifetime looking for. But that was neither here nor there. He had found Heather and the rest was inevitable.

Now, all he had to do was convince her.

Mac scowled. He had a hunch that part wasn't going to be too easy; she had a skittish look about her. He'd have to give her time to get used to the idea. A few days, at least.

Life still had a few wild cards up its sleeve, he mused, following her down the hall. Ordinarily he came to the ranch to recharge his batteries, but this time he had barely hit the property line when the hands had started flagging him down, asking if he had heard about Maude's young friend, the work she was doing on the house. They had conveniently forgotten to mention the fat farm. They had also neglected to describe Maude's young friend.

He drew to a halt beside her when Heather stopped
to open another door. Looking inside, he examined
what had once been the blue bedroom. Now, it held
two double beds and a noticeable lack of blue. He
watched Heather survey the apricot-and-cream wall-
paper and pale green bedspreads with what appeared
to be deep satisfaction.

"What do you think?" She looked over her shoulder, waving a hand toward the room.

He shrugged. "Not bad." It *wasn't* bad, but dammit, it wasn't *blue.* And there wasn't a familiar piece
of furniture in the room. "What was the matter with
it the way it was?"

"It was grungy," she said flatly. "It hadn't been
painted in years, the curtains were sun-rotted and the
rug was in pieces."

"Umm."

Straightening the ivory cloth on the bedside table,
she said, "You don't sound convinced." Her tone
clearly implied that his approval was immaterial.
Gazing quickly around the room, she gave a satisfied
nod, then came out and closed the door.

Turning, he followed her back the way they had
come, to the sitting room. One glance told him all he
needed to know. Gone were the two comfortable old
chairs with the sagging cushions, the thick drapes that
had hung there as long as he could remember, the
boot-scarred coffee table and the massive couch that
had served several generations of Mackenzies.

"You don't like it."

She was getting better, he reflected. She wasn't asking anymore. He took his time, starting at the Orien-

tal rug surrounded by gleaming oak planks, then moving to the sheer lace curtains she was fiddling with. They allowed enough sunlight in the room to strike fire in her hair and brighten the muted gold walls. The furniture was flowered and built on a small scale.

He turned back to her. "I'm still adjusting. Don't ask me to get excited about the changes. At least not yet. Okay?"

Heather's brows rose. "Okay."

"It's a far cry from what it used to be."

"I consider that a compliment."

"And definitely not a man's room."

"Another plus, considering that we cater to women."

It was almost too easy, he muted, watching exasperation narrow her eyes. Then as a sudden thought occurred to him, he frowned and took another more leisurely look around. "What happened to all the family pictures?"

Heather looked upward in silent appeal. After a moment she sighed and said, "Don't worry. I haven't made off with any of the family treasures. They've been carefully packed and stored."

"Why?"

"Why are they stored?"

"Why were they taken down?"

She stiffened. "Because portraits of men with bushy mustaches and paintings of cattle stampedes don't exactly fit into the new décor."

"I thought it was fine just the way it was."

"And you'd know, of course. Do you have a lot of time between tending horses and cows to decorate houses?'' Heather marched over to a partially filled bookcase, annoyed with herself. She rarely descended into outright unpleasantness. Yanking several books out of an open box and slamming them on a shelf, she demanded, ''If it was so great, why didn't you take care of it? No one had done a thing to this beautiful old house in years. The floors needed sanding, everything needed paint and—''

''This is a house,'' Mac reminded her. ''Not a work of art.''

Heather's expression as she gazed around the room was surprisingly revealing. Far more revealing than she would have liked, he guessed. She looked at it much as a doting parent would watch her offspring, with an unconscious gleam of possessive pride.

''You're wrong,'' she said quietly. ''A house like this was built by craftsmen, with love, and it should be treated that way, not neglected and ignored.''

Mac walked over to a small round table standing on newspapers. He picked up a large absorbant cloth and a bottle of lemon oil. ''Is this for the table?''

Heather nodded. ''That's one of today's projects.''

He unscrewed the cap on the bottle. ''I'll do this while you finish filling the bookcases.''

Surprise replaced exasperation as she considered his offer, apparently looking for his ulterior motive. Finally, she nodded again and lifted some more books out of the box. Mac dropped to one knee, sprinkled oil on a small section of the table, then smoothed it on with long strokes of the cloth.

Lining up the books on a shelf at eye level, Heather eventually broke the silence in the room. She waved a

NEVER ON SUNDAE 23

hand at the table and asked, "Why are you doing this?"

Looking up, Mac considered both the question and her puzzled expression. "It needs to be done," he said simply.

Heather sighed. "You know what I mean. You don't like anything I've done to the house, it's written all over your face. So why are you helping me?"

Rubbing a finger over the smooth oak grain, he said, "What do you expect me to do, throw a bomb at the place?"

"I don't know. But I certainly didn't expect you to pitch in and help me get it ready. Not that I don't appreciate it," she added hastily. "I do. Our first clients will be here in just two days."

"I gather that Maude told you how I'd feel." Leaning back, he watched her reach for another book and study the spine. He waited until she looked up, her brown eyes meeting his in a long, level look.

She wiped her dusty hands on her jeans. "Yes, she did—in great detail. After hearing what she had to say, I wouldn't even begin work until she pulled out the deed and convinced me that you have no legal claim on the house. I didn't want any problems over this place."

Legal. That was the operative word, Mac thought. He poured some oil on the cloth and began working on one of the legs. "Four generations of my family lived here. My great-grandfather—the first Mackenzie to live in this area—built it." He looked up just in time to catch her stretching on tiptoes to reach the top shelf. After wiping his hands, he crossed the room, plucked a small utility step stool from its place in the corner and dropped it on the floor beside her with a thud. "Why is it that women never use a stool when something's too high for them?"

"Beats me," she said with sudden cheerfulness, stepping up on it. "Undoubtedly for the same reason that a man won't stop and ask for directions. It's probably genetic. Four generations," she prompted. "What happened to them?"

Picking up the cloth, he ran his hand down the wooden leg and dabbed at a spot he'd missed. "They worked hard, married, had kids. When enough of them had come along, they built the second house." He gestured over his shoulder toward Maude's place. "After awhile, there were too many for one ranch and some of them decided that there had to be an easier way to make a living. So they moved away, a few at a time."

"Until eventually only Maude's immediate family was left here."

It wasn't a question, Mac noted, wiping the oil off with a dry cloth. Well, fair was fair, he decided. She had done her homework. He nodded. "Yeah. And as the others moved, Maude and her husband bought out their interest in the family homestead."

"Until they were sole owners." Heather propped her elbow on a shelf and waited for his reply.

"Right. No one in the family would argue about that. Everything here belongs to Maude."

"To do with as she wishes?"

Mac nodded and started on the next leg. The lady really did like to push, he mused. But then, he did his fair share of pushing, too. "Right. Maude has the right to turn the place into a circus if she wants to."

"Or a fat farm?"

He frowned, rubbing harder. "Or a fat farm."

Heather didn't bother hiding her sigh. A few seconds later she realized that her relief was a bit premature.

Mac looked at her, his lips curving in a small smile. "But I'll give you five-to-one odds that it won't last the summer."

Chapter Two

He owns a *what?*"

It was later that evening, and Maude had left Mac involved with a thriller on TV, sneaking away from her house to visit Heather and to murmur soothing noises. The living room was softly lighted by several small lamps, and the two of them sat in graceful, high backed chairs, sharing a small footstool.

Maude blinked at the stunned astonishment in Heather's voice. "A paper," she repeated in a patient tone.

"Are you seriously telling me that your cousin or nephew or whatever he is, Wade Mackenzie—"

"Mac," Maude said helpfully.

"—owns a newspaper in Colorado?" Heather uttered each word slowly and distinctly, or at least as slowly and distinctly as she could between gritted teeth.

Maude nodded, a glow of pride deepening the blue of her eyes. "A big one."

"I don't think I want to hear this." Heather leaned back in the cushioned chair, staring moodily at the older woman. He wasn't a cowboy. Even though everything from his scuffed boots and wide-brimmed hat shouted that he was, he wasn't. She should have known, Heather told herself. Although *why* she should have known, she wasn't certain. After all, Maude came from the same family and *Maude* lived on a ranch.

But she had spent the entire afternoon with him, so she should have suspected *some*thing. Then again, she argued silently, he hadn't acted like an editor—however that might be. And aside from asking pointed questions about missing items in the house, he had given a perfect imitation of the strong, silent cowboy. He had either done it deliberately, or the man was a chameleon, changing his colors to adapt to his surroundings, she decided finally.

"In Denver."

Heather focused her gaze on Maude's pleased expression. "I beg your pardon?"

"His paper. That's where it is, in Denver."

"It would be." No little one-horse town for Wade Mackenzie. Nothing but the big time.

"Of course, he doesn't exactly own the whole *thing*," Maude explained earnestly.

"Thank God for small favors," Heather murmured, knowing that she was sulking and deciding to

wallow in her bad humor. But, damn it, she didn't like
being made a fool of—especially by a smooth, smiling mountain of muscle. Her mood slipped another
notch as she reminded herself that she had recently
accomplished that particular feat with no outside help
whatsoever.

Heather's eyes narrowed as she thought of his per-
formance that afternoon. He'd known damn well the
impression he'd given when he'd drawled "Yep" and
"Nope" and fiddled with his cowboy hat. He'd encouraged her to jump to the obvious conclusion. And
she had fallen for it like a ripe plum.

"Oh my, no indeed," Maude confided. "The whole
family *owns* it. He just runs it."

"Is that all? Poor baby." Throwing all pretense of
composure to the wind, she burst out, "Then why is
he dressed up like Hopalong Cassidy and playing
cowboy? Doesn't he have anything better to do? Why
isn't he in Denver telling people to stop the press or
something?"

"Are you angry at Mac, Heather?"

The bewildered words were merely an expression of
Maude's concern, but they had the effect of a dash of
cold water on Heather. She drew in a deep breath and
exhaled slowly, shaking her head. No, she wasn't mad.
At least, not with Wade—*Mac*—Mackenzie, she admitted silently. But if the question had been phrased
differently, directed at her, her answer would have
been a sharp affirmative. He *had* deceived her.
Whether the deception was deliberate or not was a
moot question. The point was, she had fallen for it.
Again.

The man had made a fool of her. No, she amended with hard honesty, she had simply displayed her usual appalling lack of judgment when it came to the male sex. She had *allowed* herself to be deceived. Again. It was a good thing Les wasn't around, she thought with a wry smile, pressing her head back against the chair and staring at the ceiling. It hadn't even been six months since her brother had extricated her from that awkward situation and tried to drill in her the basic precepts of prudence and self-preservation. And yes, she was still smarting from the experience.

But obviously it hadn't worked.

Oh, the rescue had been a success; anything of that nature undertaken by Lester Carmichael Brandon, the heir apparent, was a success. It was the lecture that hadn't worked. She still went with her instincts—lousy as they seemed to be—and played her hunches. And Les wouldn't understand that lack of logic now, anymore than he had then. Her brother hadn't become a hotshot real-estate broker by taking people at face value.

"No," she finally said, hoping to erase Maude's worried look. "I'm not mad at Mac. Just embarrassed by the mix-up, I guess." She firmly changed the subject to one of more immediate concern. "Did he finally unpack and get settled in one of your bedrooms?"

Maude bobbed her head. "The dear boy," she said with a fond smile. "He's taken it better than I thought he would."

Heather stared at her addled friend. Taken it well? That man, who was neither dear nor a boy, was placing bets that her new business would fold before the summer was over.

"I thought for a minute that he was going to haul a bed into our new gym and stake his claim."

"It was partly my fault," Maude admitted. After a quick peek at Heather's quizzical expression, she sighed. "All right, *all* my fault. Mac always stayed in this house when he came to visit me."

Heather kicked off her sandals and wiggled her toes. "A little detail you neglected to mention when you told me how he felt about the place."

"Yes, well, I thought that if I explained it to him, he would understand. You were already having second thoughts about tackling the job, and I wanted you to get started."

"But, you *didn't* tell him."

"I was going to, but then you began the work and everything was so confused, with men coming and going and all. I just . . . lost track of the time."

Heather grinned at the other woman's doleful expression. "You're a fraud, Maude. And a con artist. Once you got me moving, you had no intention of telling him—did you?"

"Heather! Child, how can you say that?" Maude worked at looking wounded.

"Easily. Come on, admit it."

Maude's lips twitched. "Well." She drew the word out as she raised her hands in a "what can I say?" gesture.

"Hah! I knew it."

"But only because I've found that things like this always work out. I knew you would handle it. And that he would eventually calm down. You *do* understand, don't you?''

Heather nodded slowly. Yes, she understood—far more than Maude had intended her to. She also realized that Maude's statement was a clear example of her philosophy of life: someone else would eventually clear up the mess. And in this case, Heather was the designated agent. A hopelessly inept one, she was afraid.

She had originally consented to redecorate the house because that was her area of expertise. Then, somehow, she had agreed to stay on for six months—to live in the house while Maude remained in her own—to supervise the running of the place. She had, of course, expected to rely heavily on Maude's extensive business experience. And therein lay the problem, she mused. So far, Heather hadn't unearthed much in the way of entrepreneurial expertise in the older woman.

Heather had squashed the doubt that reared its head more and more frequently. Certainly Maude had a vast reservoir of knowledge to share, she'd assured herself briskly. Good heavens, the woman ran a ranch, didn't she?

Or did she?

Heather stared at Maude's placid expression and decided to quit fooling herself. If her soft hands were any indication, it had been some time since her plump friend had done any physical labor. And more than likely, she paid someone to attend to all the other details so she could live in her house when she wanted to and dash off when she got the urge to travel. Heather took another look at Maude and drew in a long, rather desperate breath, suddenly realizing the extent of her commitment. That meant that the buck stopped with *her*, that Heather Brandon, liberal arts major, was in total charge of a business. Her family, she thought abruptly, would be as surprised as she was.

While she was grappling with the ramifications of her latest insight, Maude got up and trotted to the door.

"Mac! Come in." She led him into the sitting room and beamed at Heather. "Isn't this nice?"

Heather glanced up. "Peachy."

"I thought I'd find you here." Mac wrapped his arm around Maude's shoulders and squeezed gently. He nodded at Heather, inspected each piece of furniture with resignation and finally settled his large frame carefully on the couch. Reaching into his shirt pocket, he pulled out a business card with a distinctive and colorful logo, holding it between his thumb and middle finger so they could both see it. "I saw a stack of these by the phone. Palm trees?"

Maude coughed and examined her fingernails.

Heather glared at him like a hen protecting her lone chick. "What's the matter with palm trees?"

"Not a thing." He stretched his legs out before him and considered her flushed face. "Except there aren't any within fifty miles of here. Probably more miles than that."

Heather gave him a bright smile. "There are now. We planted several last week."

He waved the card, mutely urging her to examine the image of tall, swaying palms. "Like these?"

"They're a bit smaller," she admitted.

Maude cleared her throat. "Actually, they're only about five feet tall, but they'll grow, and in years to come, they'll welcome people to The Oasis." Her buoyant smile enveloped the two of them.

Mac leaned back and glanced from one woman to the other, wondering what quirk of fate had brought the two of them together. Maude, round and no taller than her new palm trees, had the bright-eyed enthusiasm and attention span of a three-year-old. But her continuing involvement in a project was in direct ratio to the white heat of her interest. Her curiosity, optimism and constant desire for the new and unusual, which years earlier had made her his favorite relative, were precisely the traits that now drove him to distraction.

If steadfastness and sheer willingness to work were the criteria under consideration, he mused, then Heather was light-years older than Maude. She had apparently thrown herself heart-and-soul into the setup. She would have had to, in order to accomplish all that she had in such a short time. And judging by the tour he had taken that morning, Heather was also very good at what she did; even though the familiar, comfortable furniture was gone, she had retained the character and integrity of the place.

His lady seemed hell-bent on proving something. He didn't know what, but he intended to find out. He didn't even know if it was to herself or to the world at large, but since he'd already decided that he was going to stick around, he'd soon know. And while he was at it, he decided again, he was going to get rid of those wary glances she kept sliding at him.

Heather's curious gaze met and tangled with Mac's. She frowned at his sudden smile. So what was the matter with little palm trees? she wondered edgily. They'd grow. And Maude had had her heart set on them. Besides, she couldn't think of a single client who would waste time comparing the logo with the real thing. She and Maude had discussed the subject of a name for their business at length, and once they'd decided on The Oasis, Maude had pointed out with irrefutable logic that any oasis worth its salt had palm trees.

As Maude energetically lectured Mac on the rapid rate of growth one could expect from immature palms, Heather recalled her first meeting with the older woman. She had breezed into the gym in Phoenix and plunked herself down on the Exercycle next to Heather, complaining about the heat.

"I swear it gets hotter here every summer!"

Heather had smiled.

"I'm here visiting some friends, and they got me a visitor's pass," she confided chattily.

Heather nodded. This was obviously a woman who knew no strangers.

"If God is as loving as I was brought up to believe," Maude stated with a rueful look at the chunky thighs stretching the fabric of her leotard, "I would have been born to vegetarian parents. But what did I get?" She didn't wait for an answer. "Farmers—people who ate biscuits and gravy for breakfast, along with their eggs and potatoes. Starches for lunch and supper," she panted, starting to pedal in earnest. "Good solid food that stuck to our bones, and everything was fried. But I forgive them," she stated generously. "They had no idea they were creating monster fat cells for me."

She wiped a drop of sweat from the tip of her nose and inspected Heather, starting at her running shoes and working up to the French braid. "What are you doing here, honey? You one of the instructors taking a break?"

"Thighs." Heather muttered, picking up speed. "The family thighs. They refuse to fit into jeans unless I hit this place at least four times a week."

"There has to be an easier way," Maude groaned.

"Figure one out, and you'll make a fortune."

"Actually," Maude stated with certainty, "I do have one. It came to me when I was stranded at the ranch for a few days after a flash flood. It hit just before the cook's usual shopping day, and we ran out of food. Good food, that is. We were down to eating *vegetables*."

Heather grinned. Maude made it sound like they had been forced to roast field mice over an open fire.

"Celery and squash were coming out of our ears. No siree, it wasn't a laughing matter. If the hands had had a boat, they would have quit. I tell you, honey—what *is* your name? I can't keep calling you honey.... Heather? Nice name— I tell you, Heather, it gave me to think. Especially when the helicopters started buzzing around and we thought we were saved. Of course, we weren't. We went running outside in all that mud, yelling and waving and do you know what they did?"

Heather shook her head.

"They dropped hay for the horses. Not a morsel for us. What are you laughing at? This is a serious story, and it has a point. Somewhere." She frowned and pedaled slower while she thought.

"Ah!" Maude nodded briskly. "The point is that I realized for the first time exactly how isolated we were, and if I *truly* wanted to lose weight, all I had to do was stay at the house with no food—or just lots of the right *kinds* of food. What it boiled down to, though, was that I didn't want to lose weight *that* much. God forbid I should get *thin*.

Heather nodded encouragingly to the plump partridge of a woman. Maude spoke in italics and exclamation points as she artlessly rattled on, confiding everything from the state of her health to the problems of having a fifteen-thousand-acre ranch.

In response to her equally direct questions, Heather found herself being just as candid. Only once did Maude appear to be startled. When she heard Heather's last name, her silvery-gray brows shot up so high they disappeared beneath her curly bangs. "Brandon, as in *the* Brandons?" she inquired.

Heather nodded.

"To those who read the financial pages the first thing in the morning," Maude ventured, "it's a name that brings to mind circling sharks."

Heather checked the flickering red numbers by the handlebars and picked up speed. "That's right," she said, panting.

"Interesting. Did you inherit any of their skill at power plays?"

"'Fraid not. They think I'm a changeling." She grinned. "In a family full of M.B.A.'s, I'm the arty one."

"*Much* more interesting," Maude approved warmly. "What do you paint?"

"I don't. I decorate."

"Ah. What?"

"Rooms, houses."

"What are you working on now?"

"A rambling old house that a young couple bought." Heather turned to face the older woman, her brown eyes sparkling with enthusiasm. "We're converting the bottom half into a toy shop, and the upstairs will be living quarters. It's going to be a gem."

"You like old houses?" Maude asked with a thoughtful look.

"Love them, the bigger the better. Some day, I just might buy one, fix it up and open a bed-and-breakfast."

"Ah."

"These days," Heather added, blissfully ignorant of the dark machinations hovering beneath Maude's *ah*, "few families are large enough for old homes. Even if they have enough children to fill the bedrooms when they buy it, the kids grow up, move away and leave the parents rattling around in a huge place. So more and more, businesses are buying them and tastefully turning them into offices or shops."

"And you approve of that?"

Heather nodded decisively. "As long as the work is done well, I approve of anything that will keep those glorious old houses from being neglected or razed."

"Ah."

And that was when Maude had begun her campaign. Each day she returned to the gym, climbed on the bike next to Heather and like a busy terrier worrying a bone, argued her case. She had *two* houses, she informed Heather, which was clearly twice as many as any mortal needed. One of them would make a marvelous spa, a retreat, a plush bolt hole for women who wanted to leave stress and calories behind them. All Heather had to do was what she was already doing: fix up an old house for a new business. It was quite simple, really.

Heather blinked, dimly aware of the animation in Maude's voice as she continued the defense of her palm trees. She didn't allow Mac's indulgent comment to prevent her from gazing in satisfaction around the room. The house was lovely, but it hadn't been as simple as Maude had predicted. Maude had a way of jumping from concept to completion, ignoring all of the meticulous steps required in order to get from one to the other. No, she didn't actually ignore them, Heather reflected. She simply didn't recognize that they existed. She just seemed to believe that once she'd put the plan into action, her part was done.

With a sigh, Heather admitted to herself that she had taken one look at the house and fallen in love. It was a comfortable dwelling that made no pretense of being other than what it was: a large, family home. Rooms had been added onto the original structure as more babies arrived, and the large, wraparound porch had undoubtedly sheltered excited children from the rain and been the central gathering place on warm nights. Harsh weather and the passage of time had dimmed its sprawling, informal beauty, but Heather had the feeling that it had simply been biding its time, waiting for the proper person to come along and restore it to its former glory.

Heather's satisfied contemplation of the room was brought to an abrupt halt when Maude glanced at her watch and jumped to her feet.

"I'm going home. It's past my bedtime. No," she waved Mac back down to the couch. "It's much too early for you. You stay and keep Heather company. You children need to get acquainted." She trotted across the room and out the door, slamming it behind her.

Mac finally broke the silence. "You want to play marbles?"

Heather stared at him, a smile tugging at the corners of her lips. His hair was darker in lamplight than it had been in the rays of the afternoon sun, and his green eyes were frankly amused. He was an attractive man, she acknowledged silently. Too attractive. Too dangerous. She was definitely not interested. She shook her head. "No thanks. I think I lost all my marbles when I joined this business venture with Maude."

Her brother would have agreed. With the memory of Les saying in a stunned tone, "You're staying in the desert for half a year with someone you met at a *gym*?" her smile broadened. Reminding him that she was twenty-seven and had been free-lancing for some time had not soothed him. But then, she hadn't been trying very hard. Les had been a royal pain in the backside since her father retired and her parents had decided to enjoy some long overdue traveling. Les had to learn that she was competent and capable of taking care of herself—especially where her business was concerned.

But her brother was the least of her worries, she reflected after another quick glance at the man across from her. Mac was a lot closer, and even that casual sprawl and half grin couldn't conceal the predatory gleam in his eyes. Her first impression had been right; he was definitely on the prowl.

"Okay, marbles are out," he said. "How about 'Twenty Questions'?"

Heather shook her head. "I'm too tired at the end of a day for games."

"I'll make it easy on you."

She looked at him skeptically, intrigued in spite of herself. "How about forgetting the games," she told him, restless beneath his steady gaze. "You just ask me what you want to know, and I'll decide whether or not I want to tell you."

"Done. When did you rename the place? This spread has been known as Gunthers' Ranch for—"

Heather held up her hand to stop him. "Wait, let me guess. Four generations, right?" Satisfied when he frowned, she said reasonably, "A name is just as necessary for a business as it is for a newspaper, so we selected one and designed a logo for the business cards and stationery. But if you ask around in town, you'll find that nothing much has changed. Sure, the people know that Maude has a business called The Oasis, but as far as they're concerned this place is and always will be Gunthers' Ranch. And just to make sure that we're on the same wavelength, let's get one thing straight. *I* didn't change the name. Every decision has been made by mutual agreement. Believe me, I did nothing on my own."

His gaze shifted from her face and he made a deliberate survey of the room. "What about the house?"

Heather's sigh was a sound of pure exasperation. "Have you ever worked with a decorator?" she demanded. Before he could answer, she snapped, "Obviously you haven't. Look, I work like any other responsible interior decorator. I confer with my client, learn the financial framework we're dealing with, and I suggest possibilities. We discuss. If we don't come to a meeting of minds, I recommend that they find someone else."

"And if you do agree?"

"Then I get to work." She bit off the words. He was a hardheaded man who intended to nurse his grievance as long as he could, and she was tired of humoring him. "In this case, since Maude isn't living in the house, I called her in to report on the progress." And Maude had always nodded with distinct pleasure and reminded her that she was to treat the house as she would her own home. But Mac didn't need that bit of information, Heather reminded herself. He was already regarding her as if she made a habit of conning little old ladies out of their bank accounts.

"Okay." Mac got to his feet and prowled around the room, absently touching the fine oak grain of the table by the windows. He turned to face her, shoving his hands in his back pockets. "I apologize." The stunned expression on her face was almost worth the apology, he decided, watching as her shoulders slowly relaxed against the back of the chair. "You were offered a business deal and you accepted. It's not your fault that Maude didn't warn me. Nor is it your fault that I'm having a hard time handling the situation."

"Right now, I'm having a little trouble myself," Heather admitted.

"Yeah. Well, I just want you to know that I'm not always so hard to get along with. So what do you do next?" he asked.

Heather's smile was what he had been waiting for all day. Her soft laugh was a bonus.

"Tomorrow is the last day before our first guests arrive. I'm planning a nervous breakdown," she admitted.

"Are many coming?"

"Five. A full house."

"How'd they find out about a place in the middle of nowhere?"

She smiled again. "Maude, of course. Did she tell you that she met me in the gym in Phoenix?"

He shook his head, afraid that if he said anything it would be the wrong thing. She was finally talking and he didn't want her to stop.

"That was our beginning. By the end of two weeks, she not only had me signed up, she had talked most of the other women into coming here. They're lined up just waiting for us to open. The first group is even staying for two weeks."

Mac shook his head in disbelief. "I don't get it. What do you have to offer that they can't get in Phoenix? Or Tucson?"

Heather's lips curved in a satisfied smile. "That was Maude's selling point from the beginning," she explained patiently. "It's not so much what we have, it's what we *don't* have that sold the place to them. Look, what do you suppose it is that these women want to do more than anything else in the world?"

Mac ran a hand through his hair. "I can't even figure out why they'd pay the kind of money they're obviously paying—"

"No fair. Answer my question."

"Hell, I don't know what they want. To get thin, I suppose."

"According to Maude, they *talk* about getting thin, but what they really want is to eat. Of course," she added, highly entertained by his startled expression, "deep down inside of them, they know that certain foods are bad for them. They just have a terrible time resisting them. So what they're paying for is to be kept away from food."

"I think you've spent too much time around Maude," he muttered. "You're almost making this sound plausible. Are you telling me that you're not going to feed them?"

"You're a reasonable man," Heather said. "Do you honestly think we could get away with that?"

"What does reason have to do with this?" he demanded. "Are you sure these women didn't think Maude was joking, and just went along with the gag?"

Heather's pitying smile was answer enough. "We've already got their money."

"Okay, I give up. What are you going to do with them?"

"Feed them, of course. Tempting meals drawn up by a nutritionist and prepared by a fantastic cook we've hired. The only thing we won't have—and they'll have absolutely no way to get—will be the goodies that are so accessible in every town and city."

"You think it will work?"

"Of course it will. It'll be good for us," she said bracingly.

"Us?"

"Of course," she said, surprised. "I'm just as bad as they are. What do you think I was doing in the gym in the first place?" Without waiting for an answer, she admitted darkly, "Chocolate is my downfall."

Mac blinked, "Chocolate?"

She nodded. "Doesn't everyone feel that way? Don't you like it?" she demanded.

He thought about it. "Well, yeah, I suppose so. But I like vanilla and strawberry, too."

Heather got up and walked barefoot over to the window, staring out into the darkness. She wasn't talking about *liking* chocolate. What she had in mind was a devoted, unflagging, all-out love affair with it. "I think this comes under the heading of something that only a woman would understand," she complained to his reflection in the window, watching as he drew closer. "It's not just something I *like*, it's a passion."

Two large hands rested on her shoulders and his thumbs gently kneaded at the tension between her shoulders. "Well, we have a full month ahead of us. That gives me enough time to share your passion."

Chapter Three

Barney?"

Heather opened the screen door and stepped out on the porch, calling to the lanky, balding foreman. "Who's going into town tomorrow to meet our guests?" That was one thing that Maude had been right about, she mused. The nearest town was thirty miles away and half of those miles were rutted dirt roads, so the women were being transported in a 4×4.

Barney turned, tugged the wide brim of his hat down a notch, and ambled over to the house, taking a bite out of a thick, moist brownie, slathered with chocolate frosting. "'Morning, Heather," he mumbled thickly before swallowing. "I thought I'd make the first run. Need anything while I'm in town?" He bit off another chunk.

Heather's nostrils flared as she inhaled the seductive aroma produced only by chocolate, and she swallowed right along with Barney. It had to have at least a thousand calories, she decided, stoically watching him pop the last of the brownie in his mouth and lick at a dab of frosting on his thumb. And regardless of what the scientific community said about the number of calories it took to gain an ounce, on her that brownie would be at least two pounds and an inch on each thigh.

It didn't matter. She wanted one. As tired and hungry as she was, she would even consider trading her grandmother for one. She tightened her hands on the porch railing and frowned. "Did Millie bake those today?"

After wiping his hand on his jeans, Barney shook his head. "Nope."

Millie, a slim woman in her forties with dramatic slashes of silver in her dark hair, had been cooking for the ranch hands and Maude for ten years. She was known in the community for her hearty, meat-and-potatoes meals and the endless succession of desserts she served in Maude's large dining room. Six days a week, she placed pies, cobblers and cakes to cool on the broad windowsill of the roomy, old-fashioned kitchen. At first, Heather had assumed that at least one day in seven the main meal would end without dessert. Not so. Since Millie didn't bake on Sunday, she simply did double duty on Saturday.

Jodie, the chef recommended by the Oasis nutritionist, was scandalized by such irresponsible behavior. Her desserts were low-calorie, low-cholesterol

concoctions with plenty of fiber. After a steady diet of
Millie's meals, Heather told herself that she should be
looking forward to Jodie's disciplined approach to
good nutrition. But so far, she wasn't convinced.

She watched Barney's tongue catch a stray crumb at
the corner of his mouth. "Not Millie's?" she asked
again.

The foreman squinted up at her. "Nope." His lips
twitched.

Heather sat down on the top step and glared at him.
He, along with the other men, had discovered her
weakness for chocolate, and none of them was above
teasing her. She smoothed her pleated shorts over her
thighs and said, "Barney, you *do* understand what
we're doing here, don't you? At The Oasis, I mean?"

"With the women who are coming in tomorrow?"
He took his time and thought it over. "Sure. It's like
a health club. They can ride the horses, swim, go for
walks, play tennis. Your part is to keep them away
from food."

"Not *all* food. Just certain kinds. Like killer
brownies." She watched his half smile turn to a grin.
"And I don't see myself as a housemother. *I* don't
have to keep them away from food. We provide a location that does that." She eyed him severely. "But I
do have a certain responsibility to make it as easy as I
can for them. And it just dawned on me that maybe
I've overlooked something. I think you guys are going
to have to confine your eating to certain areas."

The lazy grin slipped off his face. "Whoa. Now just
a darn minute, Heather."

"Barney, I don't know how to emphasize this enough. We're dealing with women who just love food—"

His deeper voice almost overrode hers. "These men work hard, and sometimes they have to grab a bite whenever they can."

"—women who would kill for a hunk of chocolate!"

"I'm not about to tell them that they can only eat in the kitchen!"

The two of them drew to a halt at the same time, scowling at each other.

Waving her hand in a gesture that encompassed the entire ranch, Heather said, "Darn it, Barney, they've got fifteen-thousand acres to eat on. Do they have to parade around this house chewing on chocolate and—"

Barney held up his hand, palm facing her like a stop sign. Quizzical gray eyes inspected her flushed face. "I've got a box of these brownies at home," he finally said. "Do you want one?"

Heather flew down the stairs and linked her arm through his. "I thought you'd never ask," she admitted with a rueful smile, turning with him and moving toward his cabin.

It wasn't far away. As far as that went, *nothing* was far away. The two main houses were about two hundred yards apart. Midway between them and off to the side were the pool and tennis court. Set roughly four hundred yards beyond Maude's place were the bunkhouse and Barney's cabin. Beyond that was a line of paloverde trees that snaked its way across one side of the valley into the foothills.

"I'd practically trade the new hot tub on the back porch for one," she added, lengthening her stride in an attempt to match his.

He chuckled. "I figured a chocolate fit was coming on. Mary's the same way when she's feeling deprived."

"Umm. Well, it's a big club that your wife and I belong to." She nodded when he opened the door and made a gesture for her to precede him. "And that's part of what I'm trying to tell you. Our guests don't need temptation thrown in their way. That's what they're here to get away from." She followed him into the kitchen and watched expectantly while he opened a white cardboard box and extended it in her direction.

She stared down in reverent silence. "If these taste as good as they look," she finally said, "I'm in trouble." She took a bite and her eyes widened in silent appreciation. "Oh Lord, *big* trouble." She sighed. "Okay, Barney, what bakery in town sells these? Wherever it is, don't go near it when you pick up the women tomorrow."

He closed the box and tucked it back on the cupboard shelf. "It's not in town." He turned to face her, seeming to enjoy her baffled frown.

Heather took another bite and gave a small moan of pleasure. "Come on, Barney, give."

He smiled at her ecstatic expression. "When you get real desperate you can trot over to the Gottschalks' new bakery and pick up a few of these babies."

Heather drew in a deep breath and promptly choked on a chunk of walnut. *"Gottschalks?"* she whispered hoarsely when she could talk. She fended off Barney's large hand before it could land on her back again. "Are you telling me that our nearest neighbor is making these?"

Barney nodded, a half smile still curving his lips. "Along with Ethel and Cora, her neighbors on the other side."

Heather vaguely remembered the two women who had accompanied Bertha on her last visit. "And they *sell* them?"

He nodded. "They just started last week. What's the matter?" he asked, alarmed at her expression.

"Matter? *Matter?* Nothing except possible bankruptcy! Let me have another one of those brownies. Please," she added, softening her command. She folded a napkin around it, saying, "This one's for evidence. I have to go tell Maude."

"She knows."

Heather stopped at the door and looked back over her shoulder. "Maude knows about this?" she asked in disbelief.

"Yep. I met her there the other day. She was sitting outside having some strudel and coffee."

"You're kidding."

He shook his head. "It's the God's honest truth. They sell the stuff inside, but they've put some tables and chairs out on the porch for people who want to have some coffee and visit while they eat. That's where Maude was."

"My God. Right out in the open?"

He nodded. "Yeah, visiting with some people who were driving by when they saw the sign."

Heather groaned. "What sign?"

"The one Axel put out by the main road to lure in some of the tourists."

"Damn."

Barney took off his hat and rubbed his thinning hair. "Hell, Heather, I thought you knew about it. Everyone else does."

"No," she said pensively. "I didn't know." And Maude would have made darn sure *she* didn't tell her. She wouldn't have done anything that she thought would have resulted in delaying the opening of The Oasis.

"See you later, Barney. I've got to talk to Maude." She caught the door before it slammed behind her. "Oh, about tomorrow. On your way back from town, don't use the road that goes by the Gottschalks."

"It's another five miles if I go the other way," he protested.

"Barney, I don't want the women seeing that sign. Besides, five miles is nothing out here." The door slammed as she took off on a run for the big house.

"Maude, are you home?" Heather pushed the heavy oak door open, calling out at the same time. Closing it, she hesitated, waiting for her friend to answer. "Maude? Where are you?" She listened again, then rushed toward the living room, following the gasping sound of someone struggling for breath.

She dashed to the doorway and glanced hastily around the room. "My God, Maude, are you all right? *Maude?*'' All of the chairs were empty and the sound of tortured breathing came from the floor.

As she lunged forward to look over the high-backed couch, frantic thoughts raced through her mind. Call the paramedics. No it would take them forever on that tortuous, dirt road. Call for a helicopter. *How* did she call for a helicopter? Yell for Barney. What could he do? Yell for Millie. Ditto. Pray it was some crazy game, or that Maude had decided in a frenzy of remorse to burn off that strudel in one marathon exercise session.

Her heart literally in her throat, she took a peek. ''You!''

''Eighty-seven.''

Heather stared down at Mac—or rather, Mac's backside. His body was perfectly balanced between rigid toes and arms that alternately straightened and bent; his nose almost touched the polished floor each time he lowered his body. He was covered with a fine sheen of sweat and little else.

''Eighty-nine.''

At least that's what Heather thought he said. It sounded more like a grunt between gritted teeth. Kicking off her shoes, she surged over the back of the couch, she landed on the cushions and grabbed the upholstered arm so she wouldn't roll down on the straining man.

''Ninety-two.''

She glared down at him. ''Do you know that you scared the daylights out of me? Why didn't you say something?''

''Ninety-five.''

She watched his bulging biceps through narrowed eyes. "Mac! I came through that door expecting to find Maude in the throes—"

"Ninety-eight."

"—of a heart attack, and instead I find you rolling around on the floor practically naked."

"One hundred!" Mac rolled onto his back, his chest expanding as he pulled air into his lungs. He wiped his sweaty brow with a forearm, then folded his hands behind his head and smiled up at her. "Hi."

Heather crossed her legs tailor-fashion and continued to scowl down at him. "Don't you have any clothes?"

"Maude took my pants," he told her. "Said they had a hole and she wanted to patch them."

"You don't have any others?" Heather inquired politely.

"Those are my favorites. Besides," he gestured at his snug dark-blue briefs, "these cover me up as much as a bathing suit would."

Heather drew in an exasperated breath and finally allowed herself to look at him. All of him. She had already acknowledged that dressed, Wade Mackenzie was an imposing man. Clad only in knit briefs that did *not* conceal as much as a bathing suit, he was overwhelming. Every visible square inch of his gorgeous body was tan. She refused to speculate about the rest. His arms, legs, chest and an intriguing arrow down his stomach were sprinkled liberally with golden hair.

Heather realized with some surprise that she still had the wrapped brownie in her hand. She set it on her knee, then returned her gaze to Mac, trying to keep her eyes from straying below his massive shoulders. "So, do you normally roam around the house in your underwear while your pants are being fixed?" she asked coolly.

He shrugged. "I don't know. I don't usually have anyone around to fix them. But since Maude was the one who hustled me out of them in the first place, I figured that it wouldn't bother her if I filled in the time by exercising. I wasn't expecting company."

"I'm not company," she told him, her gaze brushing his chest and stomach. "At least, not yours. Where's Maude?"

"In a little cubbyhole where she has a sewing machine. She'll be back in a couple of minutes." He rolled to his side and propped his head up with his fist, contemplating the mashed bundle on her knee. "I'll bite," he finally said. "What is it?"

Heather jerked her gaze away from the elastic band of his briefs. "Disaster," she said baldly, lifting the napkin and staring at the chocolate threat.

"It's not that bad." Mac edged closer to take a better look. "A little squashed, but it looks okay to me." He broke off a corner and popped it into his mouth. "Tastes great," he told her, reaching out to snag another piece. "Fantastic. Although I have a feeling that your nutritionist wouldn't approve."

Heather slapped at his hand. "Stop it, you're eating the evidence." She blinked when his hand slid to her bare knee and cupped it. Trying to ignore the touch of his warm fingers, she said, "I didn't bake it, so you don't have to make consoling noises."

A pair of jeans sailed over the back of the couch and landed on Mac's hip. "Mac," Maude said as she stepped into the room, "when you were a tad, I must have told you that you don't entertain young women in your skivvies. If I didn't, I'm sure your mama did."

Mac fractionally increased the pressure on Heather's knee, then surged to his feet. He stepped into the pants and unhurriedly pulled up the zipper. "You're probably right," he agreed calmly. "As I remember it, you two didn't miss much."

"Wait just a minute," Heather said, glancing one to the other. She hoped she sounded more composed than she felt. She had been shaken by Barney's news more than she'd realized, and Mac's practically naked body had done nothing to calm her down. "Don't start trotting down memory lane; I need to talk to Maude."

Maude stepped over to the chair by the couch, and when she noticed the partially eaten brownie on Heather's knee, she murmured "Oh, dear" and dropped into the cushions. She picked up a magazine and fanned herself. "Uh, Heather, I meant to tell you about that." She pointed the magazine at the brownie. "Really I did."

"When, Maude? After our guests arrived and discovered the bakery?" Heather asked gently.

Mac sat at the other end of the couch, his alert gaze moving from one woman to the other.

"No, today," Maude said, a guilty, pink flush washing into her cheeks. "In fact, I was on the way over to your place when I spotted that hole in Mac's pants. I knew you wouldn't mind waiting until I fixed it. After all, it was just a little hole, and it wouldn't take much—"

Heather rested her head against the cushion and groaned. "I think I see what the problem is here. Somewhere along the way, Maude, you decided that I was a miracle worker. I don't know how to break this to you, but I'm not. Also, I've been on the receiving end of too many surprises lately." She held up a hand when the older woman's lips parted. "Like anyone else, when a problem arises, I need time—time to work out a solution, to prepare myself emotionally, whatever. And lately, time is one thing I've had precious little of."

"What's going on here?" Mac asked quietly.

"It's all my fault." Maude looked so woebegone that despite her intention to be firm, Heather smiled. "You see, Mac, the Gottschalks opened a bakery."

He looked blankly at the two of them. "And that's your fault?"

"Yes."

"Of course, it isn't," Heather said impatiently. "Maude had nothing to do with it. At least, I don't think you did," she amended, turning to the older woman. "Did you?"

"Well." Maude made three syllables out of the word, looking guiltier than ever.

"Maude, you didn't!"

"In a way."

Heather stifled a sigh. This had all the signs of being one of Maude's long stories. "What kind of way?" she asked in resignation.

"Last December—no, I think it was January—no, it was December. I remember now. December. I had been Christmas shopping, and I'd just gotten home when Bertha stopped by. It was on the fifteenth or sixteenth."

"Is the date important, Maude?"

The older woman's eyes widened. "Of course it is, because I want you to believe that it happened long before I met you and talked about opening The Oasis."

Heather reached over and patted Maude's hand. "I'll believe whatever you tell me."

Maude blinked overbright eyes, then cleared her throat. "Bertha needed someone to talk to. She and Axel had gone through a bad financial spell and she was trying to think of a way to make some money on the side. We tossed around some ideas, then I came up with a brilliant one." She looked at Heather and her silvery brows rose in mute apology.

Heather groaned. "Don't tell me, a bakery, right?"

Maude nodded. "Right. It was so obvious. Bertha's folks came from Germany, and her mother taught her to bake pastries that are absolutely sinful. Every time we have a potluck dinner, there's a stampede when everyone heads for her chocolate-nut cake. Millie's the only cook in the area who even comes close to her."

"So you suggested that she do what came naturally." When Maude shrugged, Heather added, "And how did Bertha react?"

"She seemed interested. It was something she could do at home, and she certainly didn't need any training for it. We talked about it for some time."

"Then what happened?" Heather asked quietly.

"Nothing, as far as I could tell. She never mentioned it again and I didn't want to embarrass her, so I didn't, either. In fact, I had completely forgotten about it. Then a few weeks ago I ran into her in town." She grimaced, her eyes meeting Heather's. "She was all bright-eyed with excitement and reminded me about the talk we had last winter. She thanked me for the suggestion and said that she had hired Ethel and Cora to work part-time and that the grand opening was just a week away. She also said that she'd heard I was opening a bed-and-breakfast. I didn't have the heart to tell her what we were really doing. I knew she'd feel real bad."

"Didn't have the heart," Heather repeated faintly.

"Bertha'd be real upset if she thought her business would hurt ours."

"I guess I can understand that, but why didn't you tell me about it?"

"Because I knew *you'd* be upset."

Knowing Maude's propensity for avoiding uncomfortable situations, that made perfect sense. "So what are we going to do?" she queried. That had to be the most foolish question she'd ever asked, Heather reflected. As usual, *we* wouldn't be doing anything.

"I figured you'd come up with something clever," Maude ventured after giving it some thought.

"In less than twenty-four hours? Thanks for the vote of confidence." Staring out the lace-covered window, she sorted her thoughts and reached the inevitable conclusion. "We're going to have to tell Bertha." As Maude's eyes widened in apprehension, she said firmly, "*I'll* tell Bertha."

"Why can't we let her keep on thinking we're running a bed-and-breakfast?" Maude asked cravenly.

"Because she'd be even more hurt if we didn't steer any of our guests in that direction."

"Oh, dear, I never thought about that. When are you going to tell her?"

"Right now. I'll take one of the trucks and go see just exactly what we're dealing with."

"I'll drive you." Mac's offer took her by surprise, but before she could protest he got up and headed for the door. "Give me a few minutes to clean up."

Mac was a good driver. His large hands rested competently on the steering wheel and the way he eased his silver pickup over the ruts, he made it look easy. Heather knew from experience that it wasn't. She loosened the seat belt a bit and turned to face him.

He wasn't handsome. Unfortunately for her peace of mind, the various parts that made the whole added up to far more than mere good looks. His sea-green eyes reflected sharp intelligence, and he had a disconcerting habit of studying her with unblinking intensity. His profile, which looked like it had been chiseled from warm, dark stone, was softened only by ridiculously long lashes. Despite his size he was lean and moved with the lazy, tantalizing grace of a large cat. And he had an aura of sensual challenge, a restrained masculine force potent enough to trip the danger signals buried deep within a woman—especially a woman whose track record with men showed such a lamentable lack of judgment.

"You were a lot more patient with Maude than I would have been," he said abruptly.

Heather had the feeling that his statement surprised him as much as it did her; that he had been prepared to defend Maude and had been disconcerted when the need didn't arise.

"Maude is a very special lady. She drives me crazy at times, but I wouldn't hurt her for the world."

As if her words had prompted the thought, he asked, "How much is this bakery going to hurt your business?"

"It depends on how good a job we do of hiding it."

"That bad?"

"Worse. We're supposed to shield our guests from temptation, you know. It weakens our position a bit to have the neighbors inviting everyone over to pig out on desserts."

The pickup rolled onto the main road, and it wasn't long before they passed a sign that read, *Bertha's Bakery, Coffee And Pastries*. A few minutes later they pulled into the crowded driveway and parked between two out-of-state cars.

Mac broke the silence. "Looks like the sign is pulling them in."

"Yeah," Heather agreed glumly. "It's an eye-catcher, all right. That orange fluorescent paint probably even glows in the dark."

Mac slammed his door and came around to Heather's side of the truck. "Come on, let's see what kind of poison they're serving in there." He waited until she slid down to stand beside him, then draped his arm around her shoulders and nudged her toward the house.

Tables and chairs were cozily arranged on the large white porch, flanked by several miniature trees in rustic, wooden half barrels. Heather and Mac followed a discreet sign to the side and stood aside when a young couple opened the door and came out with coffee mugs and brownies.

Heather put her hand on Mac's arm, bringing him to a halt when he gestured her inside. "You're the one who thinks vanilla and strawberry are just as good as chocolate," she reminded him, "so I'm depending on you to get me out of here before I gain ten pounds."

Stepping over the threshold, she moved halfway into the room and stopped dead, taking a deep breath. She made a whimpering sound deep in her throat that brought Mac to a stop beside her. One surprised glance told him that the expression on her face matched the sound. Ecstatic was as close as he could come to describing it. Or exalted. Exactly the expression and the small, kitten-like sound he had fantasized about as he'd tossed and turned in Maude's back bedroom the night before. But he damned well hadn't attributed her reaction to a hunk of chocolate.

"Mac! Heather!" Bertha bustled out from behind the oak counter, wiping her hands on an old-fashioned apron. She reached up to give Mac a noisy kiss on the cheek, then turned to smile at Heather. "I wondered when you would come," she said, a slight trace of her German ancestry still detectable in her speech. She waved a hand that took in the entire room. "What do you think?" she asked proudly.

Mac studied the room, appreciating the craftsmanship in the polished oak counter and cupboards. Heather inspected the pastries behind the glass barriers.

"Beautiful job," Mac told her.

"Did you make all of those?" Heather demanded, her voice tinged with awe.

Bertha beamed. "Come," she ordered, clamping a hand on each of their shoulders and prodding them closer to the counter. "You must eat. Men must keep up their strength, and all young women are too skinny. Eat! Your first order is on the house."

Mac was already shaking his head when Heather burst into speech. "Thanks Bertha, but we'll pay for our own. Mac is starved." She ignored his startled look. "In fact, you'd better get a big plate, because he wants one of those brownies, a piece of the chocolate-mousse cake, and—oh God, éclairs—one of the éclairs." She moved down the counter while Bertha artistically arranged her choices on a plate.

"Do I want anything else?" Mac muttered, moving along behind her.

"Yes," she hissed. "You want one of everything, but you're going to control yourself."

"Anything else?" Bertha asked.

"Two coffees, with cream for one," Mac told her. "And two forks."

Mac carried the plate outside, and Heather followed with the coffee. He deposited the plate on the table and stood behind Heather's chair until she was seated. By the time he moved back to his seat, Heather was toying with her fork and eyeing the plate with a predatory look.

Mac's lips twitched. "Now I know what a rabbit feels like when it spots the shadow of a low-flying hawk." He nudged the plate to the center of the small table. "Eat," he told her. "You women are all too skinny."

Heather dipped the tines of her fork into the mousse cake and popped a bite into her mouth.

"Is there any reason why you just didn't order these for yourself?" Mac asked, watching her close her eyes and give a heartfelt sigh.

Heather's eyes snapped open in surprise and she studied his face much as a scientist would an alien creature. "Of course there is!"

"Are you going to tell me about it?"

"Well, I've developed this theory about des- serts—"

"After a great deal of research?"

"After *intensive* research." She glared at him. "Are you interested in my theory or not?"

"Fascinated." He took a swallow of coffee. "Lay it on me."

"It's really quite simple," she said. "If desserts are on someone else's plate, they aren't fattening." Her fork hovered over the éclair, then separated a small wedge from the main body.

He eyed her with grave interest. "The scientific community will be glad to hear the news."

"You're supposed to be eating," she pointed out.

Mac broke off a small piece of brownie and left it on the plate. Three healthy bites took care of the rest of it. "Have you written to any medical schools about your breakthrough?"

Heather's eyes narrowed. "Don't hassle me, Mackenzie," she told him calmly before switching her attention to the mousse cake.

"Tell me more about your research." He popped the last of the éclair into his mouth.

"Actually," she admitted with a small smile, "all of the results aren't in."

"And if you had to make a statement for the press right now?"

"I guess I'd have to state that I definitely eat less when the food is on someone else's plate."

They drank their coffee, half listening to the conversations around them. The family next to them was from Idaho and the two teenagers were earnestly assuring their parents that a box of brownies would avert the danger of starvation until dinner.

Mac finished his coffee and placed the cup on the table. "Looks like Bertha has a real winner here."

"Yeah." Heather stared morosely at the bottom of her empty cup. "I guess we ought to see if she has time to talk to us."

Chapter Four

The following afternoon the two women sat on the porch swing, waiting for Barney to arrive with the first contingent of guests. Mac, his booted feet crossed on the decorative spindle rail, lounged in a wicker chair and stared out across the valley to the distant mountains.

A hot breeze stirred the bright pink verbena bordering the walk that led up to the porch. On the porch itself, potted shade plants were placed in niches and corners, adding depth and color to the crisp white surface.

Maude broke the contented silence. "Was Bertha upset?"

Heather grinned. "Stunned was more like it, I think. She understands a bed-and-breakfast, but what we're doing is beyond her. At first she felt terrible. She said that if it hadn't been for you, she would never have opened the bakery, and ruining our business was a terrible way to repay your kindness.''

"Oh, dear."

''I told her we'd manage, if she'd just promise not to mention the shop when she comes to visit. And of course she understands why she won't be seeing any of our guests as customers.''

"So she's all right now?''

"Fine," Heather said dryly. "She consoled herself by feeding me.''

"That was after you'd already sampled everything on my plate,'' Mac commented dryly.

Maude ignored him. Her eyes brightened with vicarious pleasure. "What did you have?''

Heather groaned. "She started me off with a piece of praline pie and ended by sending me home with a box of truffles.'' She saw the gleam of anticipation in the other women's eyes and added hastily, "Most of which I left with Mac.''

"Most?''

"I kept a couple for emergencies.''

Mac stretched lazily. "I can be bribed," he told Maude.

"You can pay me for fixing your pants.'' She gave the swing a nudge with her toe. "I know I said it before, Heather, but you did a wonderful job on the house.''

"Thank you. Again.'' Inclining her head, she said, "It was a jewel to work with. Thank God your ancestors liked large rooms—it would have been a crime to make any structural changes.''

"Are you nervous?" Maude asked abruptly.

"Who, me? About a little thing like waiting for our first guests?" Heather took a long breath, knowing by a subtle shift in his posture that Mac's attention had shifted from the scenery. "Yeah, I am."

"Me, too. It all seemed so different when we were in the talking stage."

Heather patted Maude's knee. "Look at it this way—if I ever open a bed-and-breakfast, the experience will stand me in good stead."

"Have you ever thought about chucking the whole idea?" Maude asked, her gaze shifting anxiously between Heather's face and the road running parallel to a windbreak of paloverde trees.

Heather nodded. "Frequently. Mostly in the dark of night, after a day when the painters didn't show up, or the plumbers called for the fourth time and said they weren't going to make it." She spotted the 4 × 4 and turned to give Maude a swift hug. "But we're going to make a success of this place, and we're going to have fun while we do it!"

Three hours later, she wasn't so sure.

With all of the advance bookings, success was reasonably certain, she reflected, but how much fun she'd have getting there was another matter.

Mac had disappeared when the five women erupted from the car, all talking at once. They were still talking: they loved the house, they loved their rooms, Barney was a dear, and what was for dinner? Where were the cowboys, and what did people do out here in the evening?

Heather closed the heavy front door behind her and curled up on the porch swing, wishing with sudden intensity that she knew where Mac was hiding. Aggravating as he was, his company was better than that of five verbal women who all talked at the same time.

A shrill whistle brought her head up. Mac gestured from the shadows of Maude's porch, his wave an invitation to join him. She didn't need a second one.

"Hi." Heather ran up the stairs and dropped in the cushioned wicker chair next to the one Mac was lounging in. A sweeping glance took in everything from his dark brown boots and jeans to the light-blue shirt that clung to his broad chest as if it had been spray-painted on. A tan hat perched on the back of his head. He looked, she decided, like someone waiting to do one of those rugged cigarette commercials. "Be warned," she told him, scooting her chair closer to the rail. "I don't ordinarily do this."

His brows rose. "Sit next to a man?"

"Run when a man whistles."

"What *do* you normally do?" His voice was lazy.

"Ignore him. The fact that I came at a dead run is just an indication of how desperate I am."

The lines at the corners of his eyes deepened. "For me?"

Cautiously eyeing his fleeting smile, she swallowed and said, "Dream on." Then in a voice as brisk and cheery as she could make it, she clarified her statement. "Desperate to be rescued."

Heather leaned back, drew in a deep breath and hoped that he couldn't see her face. She had never developed the art of concealing either her thoughts or emotions, and right now she badly wanted to disguise both. Because whether it was his lazy smile, the look of masculine appreciation that gleamed in his green eyes, or simply everything falling into place, it was at that moment she again realized that Wade Mackenzie was a dangerous man.

And that she was a susceptible woman.

How could she not have noticed something that was so appallingly obvious, she wondered in amazement, ignoring the fact that she'd been conscious of his lean presence the first instant he'd walked in on her. That didn't count. Any woman would have reacted the same way, unless she was blind—or dead.

Had he been sending these silent, sensual messages right from the beginning? Had she been so preoccupied with putting the finishing touches on the house she had missed them? Yes, she decided in silent chagrin. Yes to both of the above.

Heather closed her eyes in self-disgust. For someone who took a rather justifiable pride in her intelligence, she'd certainly missed the ball on this one. With a stir of surprise, she recognized just how tightly she'd pulled a cocoon around her emotions after Jerrold had dropped his bombshell. Brother Lester would be pleased, she decided. His lecture had worked better than either of them had realized.

But his pleasure would be mitigated if he were in the crystal-gazing business rather than real-estate; he would definitely not be thrilled if he could read her mind. Because Wade Mackenzie was far more of a threat than Jerrold had ever been. With just a smile he'd made her remember that she was a woman with all of a woman's needs, to want what she hadn't even thought of in months.

Watch it, Heather warned herself hastily, sitting up straighter. She was also a woman who had learned the hard way what happens to those who are dumb enough to play with fire. Jerrold had been a man with this same brand of charm. An attractive man who had claimed he'd needed her, a man who had finally admitted—first to her brother, then to her—that the real attraction was the Brandon money.

Mac propped his booted feet on the rail and leaned back, folding his hands behind his head. "Well, are you having fun yet?"

Heather blinked and turned to look at him. "Fun?" she asked vaguely.

"With your guests."

"I hate to admit it," she said morosely, "but it's going to be a long summer."

"Where are they now?"

"In the pool."

"Good. Then you've got some time before they start hunting for you. Get into some jeans and boots and—" his grin was wicked "—I'll take you away from all this."

Heather glanced down at her clothes. There wasn't a lot to look at. Pink blouse and shorts, sandals, and a gold chain with a small gold heart that she wore around her neck. "These are a lot cooler." There was that smile again, she thought edgily. And the deep, vertical creases in his cheeks that made her fingertips itch to touch them. "These are good running-away clothes," she decided.

"Not if you're running on a horse." He surged to his feet, took her hand and pulled her up beside him. "Meet me at the corral in ten minutes."

Back in her room, Heather lectured herself as she pulled off the shorts and stepped into light tan jeans. "You're crazy," she muttered, looking around for her boots. "This one is nothing but trouble. He practically wears a sign on his forehead saying so. The last thing in the world you need is another man messing up your life." She tugged on her boots and stood up decisively. All right, so she'd be careful. She could do that. Now that she knew he'd be tossing those heart-stopping smiles in her direction, it was simple enough. Good heavens, they were simply going for a ride. What harm could come from that? She met her eyes in the mirror and wondered who she was trying to kid. What harm? Plenty!

Ten minutes later, as they rode toward the row of towering paloverde trees, she managed to convince herself that she was overreacting. "Which way?" she asked, pulling up in the dappled shade.

Mac cast an appraising glance at her. "Since you don't have a hat, we'd better stay by the trees. Do you want to go north or south?"

Heather looked around, frowning thoughtfully. Why did men always speak in terms of compass points, she wondered, when pointing, or a simple *right* or *left*, made things perfectly clear? A sense of direction had never been one of her strong points, but since it seemed to be a firmly ingrained masculine trait, and she had grown up with brothers who pounced on every weakness, she had learned to fake it. "Which way does south take us?"

Nodding to her right, he said, "Toward the Gottschalk place."

She said firmly, "Then we go north," and urged her horse to the left. Mac fell in beside her. He sat in a saddle the way he did everything, she decided. With a minimum of fuss and a great deal of grace. His eyes were fixed on the long valley ahead, and she realized with a sense of surprise that when he wasn't deliberately aggravating her or knocking her flat with sensual messages, he was a quiet man. That was fine with her. After spending a sleepless night worrying about every conceivable disaster that could happen to their fledgling business, she could use some peace and quiet.

The soft dirt muffled the thud of the horses' hooves, and Heather gradually became attuned to the sound of leaves rustling in the breeze, the brassy exchange of the birds overhead. A hummingbird hovered near her, the whir of wings loud in the silence before it flitted off in its endless search for nectar. Heather looked up, following the spears of sunlight through the leaves, watching a hawk ride the lift of a thermal, spiraling against the blue sky.

Slowly, one by one, the taut muscles in her shoulders and the base of her neck relaxed. She drew in a deep breath, enjoying the slow release of tension. As if he had been waiting for the sound of her sigh, Mac turned toward her, his glance starting at her French braid, lingering on the gold heart that rested between the curves of her breasts, then quickly skimming over her waist, thighs and booted feet. When he finally broke their self-imposed silence, it was with a question.

"Do you really plan to have a bed-and-breakfast some day?" He reached out and lifted a low-lying branch, holding it until she passed beneath it. What he really wanted to know was why she wasn't wearing some man's ring. However, if she had been, it would have added an unnecessary complication, so he decided to be grateful for whatever favors the gods were sending his way.

"I think so. I've been planning it for a long time," she admitted with a slight shrug.

"Why?"

Her brows drew together in a small frown. "Why a bed-and-breakfast, or why have I waited so long?"

"Both." Mac waited patiently, knowing that whatever she answered, it would only be the beginning. His curiosity was almost burning a hole in him; he wanted to know everything there was to know about her. He wanted to know her dreams and what motivated them, what else she was passionate about besides chocolate; he wanted to know why there wasn't a man in her life; he wanted to know why she shot those wary little glances at him, and why until just a few minutes ago on the porch she'd been unaware that he was crowding the *no trespassing* signs she had posted all around her.

"I've always loved old houses, the spacious rooms, the craftsmanship." Her brown eyes were alight with enthusiasm when she swung around to face him. "You can't imagine the thrill it is to walk into an old, neglected house and see its potential. To know that by sanding floors and waxing wood, by selecting the proper paint and fabric, furniture and all the individual little touches, I can make that house breathe, come alive.''

Mac shifted in the saddle, silently watching her vivid face. This was the first time she had lowered her guard enough to discuss something that was important to her, and he didn't want her to stop. He was willing to discuss just about anything if it would keep that expression on her face.

He gestured back in the direction of the homestead. ''Have you done many houses like that?''

''Um-hmm, quite a few. I've acquired a rather modest reputation for the work I've done on them, so I get a lot of referrals now.''

''Then how can you afford to stay out here for six months?''

Her shrug had the unconscious assurance of one who is very good at what she does. ''If they want me badly enough, they'll wait. The decision to stay here wasn't a whim, you know. I'll be getting valuable experience, the kind I'll need to run a place of my own.''

The line of trees broke for a distance of fifty feet or so, and he waited until they were back in the shade. ''What if you decide you don't like entertaining people?''

Brown eyes met green ones in a thoughtful stare. ''Then I'll have learned something important—that I'm not cut out for the business. If that happens, I'll probably file the bed-and-breakfast idea under the heading of a good idea that didn't work. But I doubt if it will.''

"And what about a man?"

"Man?" She seemed to test the word as if she'd never heard it before.

"Man, as in the opposite sex. Is there one in your life?"

Heather's spine stiffened, and she looked straight ahead between her horse's ears. "That's really none of your business, Mac."

He supposed that he should be squelched. He wasn't. But he was in luck; she was too preoccupied to notice his smile. "I know it isn't." He didn't bother apologizing. "Why don't you indulge me anyway?"

She darted a sideways glance at him. "Why should I?"

"Because I'm a curious man, and I'll probably keep asking until I get an answer."

"Well, you're honest, even if you are aggravating."

"So why hasn't some man hightailed it down here to take you back to Phoenix?" he prodded.

Heather sighed in exasperation. "Because there isn't one. Now."

He pounced on the word. "Now? How long has it been since there *was* one?"

"Has anyone ever told you that you have the subtlety of a stampeding bull?"

He smiled, knowing that she wasn't even close to losing her temper. "Uh-huh."

"And the sensitivity of a slug?"

"That, too." He waited until she took a satisfied breath, then said, "So, how long has it been?"

"Six months." She gritted the words between her teeth.

Mac took a quick look at her pink cheeks and snapping eyes. She didn't have the look of a woman in mourning. "So how'd you get rid of him?"

"It was very simple, really." Her voice could have frozen boiling water. "He decided that he liked the family money more than he did me, and he accepted an offer my brother made him. It was contingent, of course, on ending our relationship."

"Ah," Mac said smoothly, "the serpent in Eden. I've heard of the Brandon money."

"Most people have." Heather's voice was dry.

"So did he get any of it?"

Her gasp was a small, infuriated sound. "You really do have a lot of gall."

"I know." He absently tugged his hat down. "So, did he?"

"No."

"Why not?"

Heather heaved a sigh. "Because when I learned what was going on, I told Les not to pay him."

"Les is big brother?"

"Yes." She cast him a smoldering look as she bit off the word.

"And you believed him without any proof?"

She flexed her fingers around the reins as if she'd prefer to have them wrapped around his neck. "Les is every bit as maddening as you are, but he's never lied to me."

"I thought a situation such as that called for hard evidence, like letting the woman see the idiot accept the check."

"There was no need for that," she said stiffly, then spoiled the effect of her cool little speech by asking, "How do you know he was an idiot?"

"A man who would take a bribe of any amount to leave you is a fool and deserves what he gets." His terse reply hid the relief surging through him. So that's what all of those leery little sideways glances had been about. She was now measuring all men against that jerk. His eyes narrowed thoughtfully. If Heather hadn't had the trait before, the experience had obviously taught her some measure of caution, and she was going to think twice before putting herself in a situation where she'd get those slim fingers burned again.

He watched Heather's expression go blank with surprise. She had no idea just how much of a woman she was, he realized with a jolt. The man whose tenure had ended six months ago had obviously never touched the passion simmering behind those beautiful brown eyes. In the next instant, it hit him full force. *He* wanted to be the man who brought her to flash point. He wanted more than her fingers to burn; he wanted her hot all over, crying out for him, wrapping herself around him. Needing him as much as he needed her.

Heather cleared her throat. "Don't you have any more words of wisdom for me?" she challenged. "Aren't you going to tell me how lucky I was to get rid of him?"

He shook his head. "I'm not your brother," he said deliberately. "Besides, I make a point of never giving unnecessary advice. You've already decided that you're well out of it."

"Clever man," she said lightly. "I have indeed."

And if her determined expression was any indication, she had decided a lot more than that, Mac thought grimly. She wouldn't lightly give her trust again.

He stared at the distant foothills, frowning. Well, that was just too damned bad. She couldn't live in a cocoon the rest of her life. The day would come when it would crack wide open, and when it did he was going to be right there. When her tantalizing, lush little body fell, it would be right into his arms.

Chapter Five

The next day after dinner Heather found the guests by the pool, sitting in the lounge chairs, talking.

Not surprising, Heather reflected. The only time the women seemed to stop talking was when they were sleeping. All five of them smiled a welcome that faded around the edges when she called out, "Hi, anyone want to go riding tomorrow?"

Lou, a statuesque blonde, looked doubtful. "In a pickup?" she asked hopefully.

"On a horse." Heather grinned at the woman who was at least partially responsible for the fact that she and Maude were business partners. Lou had been the woman in the gym that day three months earlier, lamenting the hot fudge sundae and thereby reminding Maude of her plans for a desert getaway.

The other women stirred uneasily.

"Horse?" Gini asked. The tall brunette sounded as if she were inquiring about an alien creature.

Heather nodded. "That's what they were called the last time I checked."

Susan looked even more doubtful than Lou. "I don't know. I tried it once."

"What happened?" Jill and Chris asked at the same time. Both women had shoulder-length hair, but that was the only similarity. While Jill's hair was much darker than Chris's ash-brown, the main difference lay in their personalities. Chris was an observer, the quietest one in the group. Jill was not.

"The horse spent the entire time trying to have my knee for lunch," Susan said.

"We don't have a carnivorous one in the bunch," Heather told her bracingly. "Why don't you come down to the corral and take a look?" They all seemed so skittish that she added hastily, "I'd also like you to meet some of the men, at least the ones who'll be helping you with the horses." Wondering why on earth any of them had come to a ranch if they were so leery about riding, she shepherded them away from the pool and across the grassy knoll.

Barney stood near the corral gate, talking to Leo and Jim, the two young college students who would share the task of saddling horses for the women. One of them would also accompany the guests on their rides for the first couple of days, or until the women felt comfortable on their own. Because of the merciless afternoon heat, Barney had suggested that the women ride only in the morning and early evening.

That arrangement also had the merit of keeping disruption to the men's work at a minimum.

Barney had promised to talk to the two men, impressing upon them the importance of concealing the presence of the bakery. As Heather urged the five women nearer, she felt the apprehensive flutter of her stomach and hoped that he'd remembered.

Turning to face them, Barney tugged at his hat and murmured, "Heather. Ladies, I'd like you to meet Jim and Leo." When the introductions were over and the conversation turned to horses, Heather tugged at Barney's elbow.

"Did you tell them?" she whispered, drawing him aside.

"Yeah." He watched the lanky redhead lead one of the horses over to the women. "Leo has a good head on his shoulders. He's also a business major, so he understands." He nodded at the smaller, compact man. "Jim *says* he does, but he's kind of a rattle-brained kid, so I don't know. I'd feel better if we had one of the other men on the job."

As Heather's gaze moved from the younger men back to Barney, she realized that she hadn't been entirely open with the foreman and that he deserved more than half the truth. Hoping she didn't look as foolish as she felt, she said, "Uh, Barney, I know that when Maude and I asked for Leo and Jim, you had several objections, primarily their youth."

"And you said that was exactly why you wanted them."

He still sounded disgruntled, she noted. Actually, annoyed was more like it.

"Those of us over thirty are still able to lift a saddle, you know."

She eyed him in amazement. "Do you think *that's* the reason we asked for these kids? Because we thought you guys were over the hill?"

"What else?"

"Oh, Lord," she said in disgust. "That wasn't it at all."

"So tell me. I'm listening."

Cowboys of any age seemed unable to stand for more than a minute without propping themselves up, she thought absently, watching him lean back and rest his shoulders against the fence as he hooked the heel of his boot on the lower rail. "You'll probably think I'm crazy," she warned.

Barney grinned down at her. "I already thought that, when I heard why you were fixing up the house." He crossed his arms on his chest and waited.

"Well, it's just that most of the women coming here are married."

He waited a beat, then said, "And?"

"And we didn't want any problems," she finished in an embarrassed rush.

"My men don't cause problems," he said flatly.

Heather sighed. "We know that. It's the women we're worried about."

"They don't bother women, either. At least," he added honestly, "not the ones on our property."

Heather groaned. "That's not what I mean. Barney, most of the women have quite a bit of money—" She stopped when he bristled. "Now, don't get up on your high horse. I'm not accusing the men of any-

thing. If you'll just listen, you'll see what I'm getting
at. Where was I?" she asked distractedly.

"Money."

"Right. And they're bored. The women, I mean."
She watched his eyes, waiting for a glimmer of understanding. When it didn't appear, she plowed on. "And
there's something about cowboys that women find..."
She stopped, searching for the right word.

"Unpleasant?" he suggested dryly.

She shook her head. If it were only that easy. "Interesting," she ventured.

He stared, his eyes narrowing. "Too interesting,
maybe?"

"Exactly. You might almost say attractive.
Even...intriguing."

"Intriguing?"

She watched the speculative gleam in his eyes
deepen. "Definitely."

His brows shot up. "Is there more?"

Trying to ignore his half grin, she said succinctly,
"Yes. Sexy."

"*Sexy?*" Barney surged away from the fence, but
when his boot heel caught on the rail, he came to a halt
midstep, flailing his arms in the air to maintain his
balance.

"Will you be still?" she hissed, stepping forward so
he could use her shoulder as a crutch. "Everyone's
looking at us."

Barney gave a small wave to the group clustered
around the horses. His strangled whisper so near her
ear almost deafened her. "Are you saying that you

don't want any of the men around because they're *sex symbols*?''

His small grin had become a broad smile, she noted disgustedly. "Some women," she said carefully, "find cowboys very sexy." And darned if she could explain it. She wished she could, but unfortunately she had fallen right in the middle of that particular category. At least as far as one cowboy, who was actually an editor, was concerned. What he did to a pair of jeans should be declared illegal, she reflected. And those spray-painted shirts were just as bad. She wondered for a moment how he dressed for work in Denver, then wryly decided that Mac in the leashed power of a dark suit would be just as potent as he was in a pair of Levi's.

Barney propped himself on the fence again, still murmuring. "I'll be damned, well and truly."

"You probably will," she muttered, "if you don't get that satisfied smirk off your face. Pride, in case you've forgotten, is one of the seven deadly sins. The biggest one."

"A sex symbol! Hmph. Imagine that."

"We have," Heather said dryly. "That's why we asked for the kids."

"Well, if that don't beat all," he murmured, gazing off into the distance.

"Barney," she warned, "don't get carried away with this, okay? It's just a precaution, but it's one that Maude and I considered necessary. We don't want this place to get a reputation for breaking up marriages. We promised these women a refuge from temptation, and we decided that meant *all* temptation."

His lips twitched again and pure male satisfaction gleamed in his eyes. He was detaching himself from the fence when Leo called out to him. "Hey, Barney, what do you think of Atlas for Susan?"

Heather and the foreman joined them just in time to hear Susan say earnestly, "Look, guys, you really don't have to worry about me."

Jim brushed his dark hair out of his face. "Hey, Sue, this Atlas is great. He wouldn't hurt a fly."

"How does he feel about knees?" she muttered.

He ran his hand down the horse's front legs. "No problems there," he assured her.

Accepting the inevitable, the women gingerly patted the horses assigned to them. "Has anyone figured out how we get on the beasts?" Gini asked, eyeing the large back that was higher than her shoulders.

"No problem," Jim told her, nodding at a tree stump. "Just lead 'em up to that and you've got it made."

Lou looked around. "Where's the best place to ride?"

Barney pointed to the line of paloverdes. "There's a nice trail that follows the trees. Just remember to go that way." He swung his arm in a northerly direction.

"Why?" Jill asked. "What's the matter with the other way?"

The three men spoke at the same time.

"Bobcats."

"Kangaroo rats."

"Rattlers."

"Good grief, I'm sorry I asked." After reflecting on that, she said, "That doesn't make sense. All those horrors are that way," she pointed south, "but not the other?"

The men nodded.

"Why?"

Jim and Leo got busy shooing the horses away. "You tell them, Barney," they said together.

The women looked expectantly at the foreman.

After shoving his hat to the back of his head, he looked sideways at Heather. She gave a small shrug. "Because of the..." he gazed upward for inspiration. Finding none, he glanced at the waiting women. Behind him, one of the men pulled a pickup over to the barn and cut the motor. "Traffic," he said triumphantly. "We use that trail a lot, and animals just naturally head for quieter spots." Without waiting for their reaction, he lifted his hat a fraction and said, "'Scuse me, ladies. I think my supper's ready."

"Hmm. I don't know," Jill said, watching him move with the speed of a much younger man. "What do you gals think?"

"I think I don't like rattlesnakes or any of the other stuff," Susan told them, "and I'm going that way." She pointed away from the Gottschalks'.

"Sounds good to me," Gini said as the others nodded in agreement. They turned and walked back to the house, idly discussing what to wear for the ride.

Lou interrupted the conversation with a reverent, "My God." One by one they turned to her, only to find her staring at Maude's house. But it was neither the house nor the small, grassy knoll in front of the house that drew her attention. It was Mac, standing on the slight mound, watching the sunset. Unmoving, he stood with his hands tucked in his back pockets, silhouetted against the blood-red sky. A broad-shouldered and slim-hipped shadow, he was the essence of masculine grace, the sum total of all that had drawn women to men since the beginning of time.

The women halted, silently absorbing the sheer masculine beauty, the strength that matched nature's dark power around him. As the sun slipped farther behind the mountains, they moved away.

Lou finally broke the thoughtful silence. "Heather, who is that fabulous man?"

"Remember you're a married woman, Lou."

The blonde looked back. "My husband and I have this agreement. We allow each other to look. And fantasize a little. Who *is* he?"

"Maude's cousin or something," Heather replied vaguely. "His name is Mac."

"Does he live here?"

Heather shook her head. "No, he's just spending some time with Maude."

"Is he yours?"

Heather looked at her, speechless. Finally, she said, "Do I look masochistic?"

"No. But you don't look like a fool, either."

Shaking her head, Heather said, "That's exactly why he isn't mine."

The lights were on in the kitchen and as they walked by Maude's house, Millie looked out the window and waved.

"Do you know what they had for dinner tonight?" Lou asked dreamily.

Heather's smile stiffened. She could feel trouble coming. Lou was definitely a potential problem. What was worse, she was a problem with leadership qualities. A woman who could incite the troops to mutiny, especially if she caught the aroma of chocolate on the horizon.

"What *who* had for dinner?" chorused Gini and Chris.

"The men." Lou waved at the house. "The ones who eat there."

"What?"

"Pork chops and fried potatoes."

"*Fried* pork chops?" Jill stopped walking and put her hand over her heart, her dark eyes round with yearning.

Lou nodded.

"Oh, God, I haven't had one of those in a thousand years."

"And there was an apple pie cooling on the windowsill this morning."

Heather watched as the women exchanged martyred glances. "I thought you like Jodie's cooking," she said, deliberately keeping her voice serene. "You've certainly raved about it enough."

Lou patted her shoulder and said soothingly, "The meals are wonderful, Heather. Jodie's a great chef. But we're talking *fried* pork chops and potatoes here."

Heather smiled absently. The women had too much time on their hands, she reflected. The one thing she and Maude had not discussed—hadn't even considered—was providing some diversion in the evenings. They had assumed that since the women were married and generally run ragged providing for husbands and children, they would appreciate quiet evenings.

Apparently, they had thought wrong.

She had never considered the matter before, but now she realized why spas had guest speakers or some form of entertainment in the evenings: to keep the inmates from breaking out. Of course, she and Maude had a definite advantage because of their location—these women had no place to go. Except maybe to Maude's, where Millie's leftover desserts would seem like manna from heaven. Or the bunkhouse, where a refrigerator was stocked with beer and cupboards bulged with packages of cookies and chips. Heather shuddered.

So far, the women had kept busy, generally exhausting themselves with tennis during the cool hours and swimming later in the day, but she had a strong feeling that they were getting restless. And she had learned at the gym that when food was the main topic of conversation, trouble wasn't far away.

"Does she always cook like that?" Five awed faces turned to Heather.

"Millie?" She nodded. "'Fraid so." When their eyes gleamed with interest, she added in a dampening voice, "But they're hearty, meat-and-potatoes meals, full of starch and carbohydrates. You wouldn't like them at all."

It didn't take a giant intellect to realize that she hadn't convinced them, she decided a moment later.

"She bakes desserts every day?"

It was almost like watching five salivating puppies, Heather thought as she nodded, deciding quickly that honesty was still the best policy—especially when the facts could be found on the windowsill. "Every day, because there's never any left over. The men eat like a pack of wolves."

"Well," Lou consoled the others. "At least we can go by and smell them."

Fortunately for Heather's peace of mind, the conversation drifted to other matters. As the women all belonged to the gym where Heather and Maude had become acquainted, they had more in common than most people who gathered at spas.

"What do you think of the new instructor at the gym?" Jill asked, tossing the question out for general consumption.

"I like her," Lou said decisively. "I thought she made some good points when she talked about setting goals."

Susan stepped over a clump of weeds. "I've heard more about goals in the month she's been with us than I have in the last two years."

"Well?" Lou challenged. "Have you done anything about setting them?"

Susan shrugged. "Don't rush me. I'm working on it." She looked at the other woman curiously. "Have you?"

Lou nodded. "Some. I decided on several the very day she talked to us, and I've managed to meet a few of them. I change them or update them on a fairly regular basis. As a matter of fact," she added with a thoughtful expression, "I just set another one today."

"What?"

Lou smiled mysteriously. "I'll tell you when I make it."

"I don't know," Gini said dubiously. "Do you really believe they affect us that much? I'm not sure I go along with this positive-thinking theory. It sounds too pat to me, almost like a form of self-hypnosis."

Chris shook her head. "You're missing the whole point," she protested. "It's not that at all. It's more like having tunnel vision."

"I think you're on my side of the argument," Gini said dryly. "Tunnel vision sounds as bad as self-hypnosis."

"No, I didn't mean it that way. When you have a goal, it keeps you on target. You don't get distracted and go running off in a hundred different directions."

They were still arguing when they reached the house.

Heather picked up the mail that she had dropped on the hall table earlier that day and said, "I have some work to do, so I'll see you in the morning." Once she closed her bedroom door, she tossed the mail on the bed and stepped over to the window.

Now what? she wondered. It was going to be a long evening. The only reason she'd left the others was to reinforce the decision she'd made long before the house was ready. Once she had agreed to manage The Oasis, she had coped with a moment of pure panic, knowing that she would grow to resent a restrictive situation, that she wouldn't do well as a house-mother, on call every minute of the day and night. With that in mind, she'd hired Mary, Barney's wife,

to serve the meals, and composed a letter explaining
that the guests were invited to make this their home for
the duration of their stay. She had described the out-
door activities, the small library and the den with
television, VCR and a supply of films available.

Once she'd mailed a copy to each of the prospec-
tive guests—and hadn't been inundated with cancel-
lations—her waning enthusiasm for the project had
returned. Now, staring out the window, Heather knew
she had been right. After all, she told herself optimistically, if this were her bed-and-breakfast, they
wouldn't expect her to be a combined tour guide and
cheerleader as well as a hostess. No, the decision had
been made. All she had to do was stick with it.

Walking into her small sitting room-cum-office, she
picked up a magazine on window treatments that she
had promised herself the time to read and settled down
in a high-backed, generously cushioned chair.

Maude, in one of her rare moods of practicality, had
suggested the extra room. None of Heather's objections had swayed her. "You'll need it," she'd said
emphatically. After just two days of guests occupying
the rest of the house, Heather agreed.

Three hours later, Heather reached for the handrail
of the ladder at the deep end of the pool and found her
wrist clasped by a large, warm, masculine hand.

She gasped and looked up into gleaming eyes that
were colorless in the dark. "Mac! You scared the life
out of me. What are you doing out here?"

He plucked her out of the water with an ease she
envied and set her on her feet. "Here. Take this."

The hot, dry air made a towel unnecessary, but she took it anyway, wiping her face and hair, then wrapping it around her sarong-style, her hands faltering when she looked up and met his deeply appreciative gaze.

"I saw the lights and came out to see if someone had forgotten to turn them off," he said calmly, matching his stride to hers as they walked over to the table where she'd left her things.

Heather looked at him suspiciously. She had deliberately left most of them off, using only a couple of the muted pool lights. Aside from that, she couldn't think of one section of Maude's house that was visible through the surrounding trees and shrubbery. "Pretty good eyesight," she commented dryly, casting a deliberate glance at the dense foliage.

"I was out for a walk." Mac eyed her skeptical expression and grinned. She didn't believe him. Clever lady. There was nothing accidental about the meeting. He had wanted to find her and he had. This was new for him, needing to be with a particular woman, feeling her absence after just an hour or two. Of course, Heather wasn't just any woman, he reflected. The top of her head barely reached his shoulders and she was about eighty pounds lighter, but anyone who could take on Maude and survive had the spirit and nerve of an Amazon. She'd probably never back away from a challenge, either. Her way of handling a tight situation would be to stick out her stubborn chin and take the offensive. Yes, it was going to be an interesting thirty days he decided, pulling out a chair for her.

She felt it, too, he mused. Otherwise she wouldn't be wrapped like a mummy in that towel. He wondered fleetingly if she really thought it was any protection. When the time was right, a towel and a skimpy bathing suit wouldn't stop what was going to happen. Hell, as far as that went, a full suit of armor wouldn't slow them down. Because when it happened she was going to want it as much as he did, and she would be every bit as impatient as he was.

Chapter Six

W hat's that?" Mac tilted his head to read the printed logo on the letter lying in the circle of light cast by the flickering candle. "Some newspaper trying to sell you a subscription?"

Heather shook her head absently, most of her attention on the folds of her thick terry sarong, wishing she hadn't been so quick to accept the towel. The hot, dry air had already sucked the moisture from it, and she was stifling. It had been an instinctive reaction, a feeble shield against the gleam in those blasted eyes, and now she either had to shed a few yards of fabric while he watched every move she made or continue to melt.

Cursing herself for dithering, she stood up, unwound the towel and draped it over a nearby chair. The slight breeze on her damp suit almost compensated for the jolt she received when Mac's green gaze was transferred to her. Almost. He made a thorough head-to-toe inspection, reversed it, lingered on the flare of her hips, then moved up, slowly.

Drawing a slightly unsteady breath, Heather sat down. It wasn't offensive, that look of sheer masculine appreciation. It was just ... nerve-racking, especially to someone whose faith in the male half of the population had suffered a severe setback. After all, Heather reflected, it wasn't every day that one had the humiliating experience of being made a fool of—complete with witnesses—by a perfectly ordinary man. Nor was it surprising that her trusting mechanism was on the shaky side. She was definitely in no condition to deal with another male right now, especially one who was far from ordinary, one who fairly simmered with masculine hormones.

Life was not fair she reflected darkly, reaching for the letter that Mac found so interesting. "It came in the mail today," she told him, scanning the contents with a frown. "And frankly I think he's kidding."

"Who is?"

"The editor."

"About what?"

"About this." She shook the paper. "They want me to write an article for them, for their Sunday magazine section."

"About what?" he repeated patiently.

"Converting the ranch house into a business."

"May I?" He held out his hand and waited until she passed him the letter. "Looks pretty straightforward to me," he said, looking up. "What's the problem?"

Heather swatted at a mosquito. "The problem," she told him, "is that I'm not a writer. I decorate houses, remember?"

"You could do both."

"I don't know. I haven't written anything besides reports since my college journalism class."

His brows rose. "Journalism? You have hidden talent?"

"Don't get excited. It was one semester."

"There's nothing to it."

"Easy for you to say," she grumbled. "You're in the business. I don't even remember where to begin."

"With a hook."

"A what?" Heather blinked owlishly.

"The thing that catches the reader's interest," he amplified.

The look she slid at him was full of doubt. "Oh, yeah. If I remember right, that was always the hardest part. Maybe I'll just write and tell them I'll pass on this one." She held out her hand and waggled her fingers.

Mac read the letter again. When he looked up, she was frowning impatiently. "Why don't you think about it," he suggested idly, sliding it across the table. "Give it a try. It's a good policy to keep your options open."

"It's been too long. I wouldn't have the foggiest idea what to do first."

"You call them and say you might be interested and request a few sample copies of the magazine."

"And when I get them?"

His sigh sounded long-suffering. "You read them."

"I gathered that. What happens *after* I read them?"

"You analyze them. You find out how long the articles are and if they use photos, things like that. Then you examine their style, see if they're laid-back and chatty, first-person experiential or brisk and informative.

"Oh, Lord, it's all coming back," she groaned. "Then what?"

"When you're done, you ask yourself if you could write a piece like that."

"And if I say yes?"

He smiled slowly and held up a finger. "You start writing." A second finger joined the first. "And you thank God that there's an editor on the premises."

Heather examined his bland expression. "Are you offering to help?"

"Sounds that way."

"Hmm."

Mac relaxed as he watched her expression change from budding interest to outright speculation. Somewhere along the way, he had gained a reputation for being in the right place at the right time, and he had a feeling that this was one of the times that counted. It couldn't have fallen in place better if he had planned it. And if Heather's thoughtful expression was any indication, she was apparently no more immune to the lure of writing than most of the general public. It seemed to be a deep-seated belief in most individuals—including some illiterates—that they could write better material than paid staff writers. Unfortunately, sometimes they could. If she fell into the aspiring-writer category, he had it made—the perfect reason for spending time with her without coming on like Tarzan.

Those two days before the women arrived had spoiled him, he admitted silently, watching her absentmindedly toy with the tawny braid that fell over one shoulder. Having her to himself, watching her fuss over flowers, adding the feminine touches that made a house a home had touched something deep and primitive within him. He wanted her in his house, arranging his flowers, welcoming him with a smile, bringing her warmth and laughter to his bed. Dammit, he wanted *her*.

Right now she was as busy considering the pros and cons of this new venture as he was, undoubtedly wondering how it would affect her in the months to come. There was just one difference between them, he reflected. One that gave him a big advantage. *She* didn't know what she wanted.

Mac stretched his legs, carefully avoiding her bare feet, and stared at his dusty boots. Of course if she could actually write, so much the better. He had meant what he'd said about keeping options open. This could be the opportunity of a lifetime for her. Several articles placed in strategic trade magazines could impact her career in a number of ways. He gave her a few minutes, then said, "What do you think?"

"It sounds interesting," she allowed cautiously. But when she added uncertainly, "I don't know how much time I'd have to work on it," he nodded and changed the subject.

* * *

The next morning, Heather called the newspaper and requested copies of several back issues of the magazine section. Just as she replaced the receiver, her guests returned from their morning ride. She looked through the sheer curtains, watching as Leo led the group right up to the porch and helped the women dismount. If the cheerful chatter and laughing comments were any measurement, she reflected, the ride had been a roaring success.

"'Bye, Leo. See you in the morning."

"Take care of that darling horse!"

"Too bad we couldn't have stayed out longer."

From her vantage point, Heather could see the cluster of women walk in and slam the door behind them. One quick glance at their faces kept her right where she was, out of sight, unwilling to step forward and break the sudden, ominous silence.

"Dear God," Lou said piously, "take me now and put me out of my misery."

All five of them leaned back against the wall. Automatically, they adjusted their positions so the pressure was against their shoulders and not their bottoms. They were not happy campers.

Susan glared at Jill. "You wish we could have stayed longer?"

The dark-haired woman shrugged, then winced. Rubbing her derriere, she said, "I had to say something. He worked so hard to make the ride interesting."

"Too hard. I didn't need to see every acre of the ranch."

"Or the foothills," Lou moaned. "I was perfectly willing to look at them from the trail."

"How long were we out there?" Chris asked faintly.

Gini's grim voice was barely audible. "Three... hours. Three *long* hours on those wretched animals. I may never move again."

Lou groaned. "Ladies, if—and I say this with grave reservations—*if* we can make it to the hot tub, we just may live."

An expression of pure horror crossed Gini's face. "*Walk?* My legs feel like a sprung wishbone. I may never move again. Right now, even if I was invited to share one of those lunches Leo was talking about, I couldn't get my feet moving."

Jill cautiously edged away from the wall. "What lunches?"

As usual, Heather noted, the subject of food had a reviving effect on the women. One by one, they were peeling themselves off the wall and following Lou's faltering progress down the hall.

"Didn't you hear him? He was telling us how Maggie packs these enormous lunches when any of the guys is working out on the south forty."

"What does she put in them?"

Their voices faded with mutters of "roast beef sandwiches" and "apple pie."

Heather stood in the hallway, watching the walking wounded. She was torn between following with some liniment and the craven impulse to stay right where she was. The decision was taken out of her hands by the thud of booted feet on the front porch followed by a brisk knock.

She threw open the door and blinked up at a man in a blinding red shirt. Steve Jackson had dark hair, was in his mid-thirties, and had the deep tan common to all the ranch hands. He was a quiet man and Heather estimated that she hadn't spoken more than a dozen words to him in all the time she'd been at the ranch.

"Hi, Steve," she said, startled as much by the fact that he was standing on her porch as she was by the vivid shirt.

"'Morning, Heather." Steve pressed a large hand against the doorjamb and smiled down at her. "I'm going into town in a little while and thought I'd check to see if you or your guests need anything." His gaze lifted and inspected the hallway behind her.

"Shh!" Heather closed the door behind her.

"What's the matter?" Startled, he jerked his hand out of the way.

"I don't want them to hear you."

"Why?" He looked astounded. "Did I say something wrong?"

"No, it's not that. It's just that I don't want…" Her voice faded as visions of women stampeding down the hall to place orders for pizza flashed through her mind. Of course given their present fragile condition, it might be more of a hobble than stampede, but she wasn't taking any chances. "Have you ever had a weight problem?" she asked abruptly.

Steve looked startled then shook his head. Lifting a package of cigarettes half out of his shirt pocket, he said, "I've got enough grief with these things. I don't need any more problems."

"Ever tried to quit?"

Puzzled, he nodded. "'Sure. 'Bout a hundred times, but pretty soon I'd bum one off the other guys and I'd be right back on them."

"Then you know what it's like fighting a craving for something." Encouraged by his nod he said, "That's what this place is all about. We're giving them a place where they won't be tempted."

He nudged his hat back. "Well the Gottschalks played merry hell with that idea, didn't they?"

"*Shh!*"

He lowered his voice and looked around. "They can't hear me through that thick door."

"They'd better not," Heather said grimly. "They don't know about the place and I don't want them finding out."

"Would they go over there if they knew? I mean, if they're really serious about this—"

"Of course, they're serious," Heather interrupted briskly. "They're paying good money to come here." And would they go visit the Gottschalks if they learned about the bakery? Of course they would. Then they'd have a fit of remorse and try to banish the calories with exercise. On top of that, they'd feel bad, which was exactly what she was trying to prevent. "But my job is to make it easier for them, so we don't throw temptation in their way. We don't talk about food—"

His raised brows expressed his disbelief. "How can you help it? That's all *they* talk about. Hell, Heather, they know more about our meals than we do. They ask us what we had for breakfast, speculate on what we'll get for lunch, then meet us at the corral and *tell* us what we're going to have for dinner."

"You're kidding."

He shook his head, grinning.

"Oh, Steve, I'm sorry."

He shrugged, still smiling. "Actually, it's kind of funny. And Millie thinks it's great. She hasn't had this much attention since her peach cobbler won first place at the fair."

"Millie?" Heather stifled a groan.

"Sure. Your ladies walk by the kitchen at least a dozen times a day, sniffing at whatever Millie's got cooling on the windowsill and asking her what's on the menu. Well," he tugged at the brim of his hat and moved toward the stairs, "if I can't get anything for you, I'll be on my way."

"Thanks, Steve," Heather said distractedly, her gaze fixed on a second man heading in her direction. Big John was the ranch handyman; his job covered everything from patching screen to repairing the tractors. There was no mystery about his name. He was tall, had the brawny arms and shoulders of a blacksmith and was one of the busiest men on the ranch.

"'Morning, Heather." He lifted his hat off his thinning blond hair and smiled.

Heather stared. Big John, an easygoing man, smiled a lot, so it wasn't the grin that was particularly surprising. What held her speechless was his pristine appearance. Big John's job was by its nature a dirty one and he was usually smeared with a combination of grease and dust. Today he was in a flashy turquoise shirt and immaculate, fawn-colored jeans.

"I just came by to make sure that everything's okay in the house."

She considered him thoughtfully. "As far as I know," she finally said.

"No plumbing problems?"

Heather shook her head. "Everything seems to be working fine," she said, wondering at the flash of disappointment that crossed his face.

"The air conditioner?" he persevered.

"It's fine, too," she assured him.

"The appliances?"

"Most of them are new; they'd better be all right. What's the matter, John?" she asked, grinning back at him. "Did the impossible happen? Have you finally caught up with all your work?"

He shifted from one booted foot to the other. "Doubt if that'll ever happen. It's just that, uh, Maude wants everything to be nice for the guests and I, uh, thought I'd check."

"Thank you," Heather said gently, trying not to stare at the neon shade of his shirt. "I appreciate it and I know Maude will, too."

"Any time," he muttered, his ruddy face growing redder. "Just...thought I ought to check," he repeated lamely, tipping his hat and moving away from the porch.

Heather's puzzled glance followed him until he disappeared behind the screen of trees separating the house from the barn. Giving a slight shrug she slid on her sunglasses and headed for Maude's house, following the erratic path of the shade trees. The brassy sun gave fair warning of the day's heat, and she wasn't about to risk sunstroke.

Drawn around to the side of the house by the thunk of an ax biting deep into wood, Heather turned the corner just as Mac exchanged an ax for a wedge and sledgehammer. The area was littered with smaller pieces, so she assumed that he had been hard at it for some time. Sweat darkened a patch of his work shirt between his shoulders and the light blue fabric clung like a second skin.

With smooth, economical movements that told her he was no stranger to the task, he tapped the wedge into a large log. Once it was firmly in place, he backed up and took a powerful swing. And just that quickly the rhythm was established. Just that easily it was sustained.

Heather moved closer. With a small thrill of shock, she realized just exactly how powerful he was. Another realization followed the first: Mac dealt with his strength in a very understated way. He had no need to flaunt it or to flex his muscles. And somehow his easy acceptance of his smooth, powerful body made it less of a threat.

She had sensed his power on a subconscious level the day he'd controlled the pickup on the deeply rutted road, but somehow this was different. She felt as if she were watching a man who could have lived a hundred years earlier, working with basic tools, pitting his strength against the elements and winning. She had a feeling that there was a definite resemblance between Mac and the ancestors who had once worked this same land, building the two houses that remained as a legacy of their craftsmanship.

She moved forward, stopping only when he glanced up. "Have you heard something on the weather report that I missed? Should I be back at the house preparing for a storm?"

His grin was a swift slash of white. Dropping the sledgehammer, he picked up a small towel and wiped his face and neck. "Nope. You shouldn't be anywhere except right here."

He walked over to a low, split-rail fence in the shade of a cottonwood tree and sat on it, resting one booted foot on a log. Heather followed, watching him reach for a thermal jug and pour himself a glass of water. He offered it to her and waited until she shook her head before he drank.

"All right," she said, moving closer, "I give up. If we're not getting ready for a cold spell, why are you doing this in the middle of summer, in all this heat?"

"Because that's when I'm here," he said simply, running his fingers through his blond hair, then brushing particles of wood off his shoulders.

"You know," Heather said slowly, assessing him with a puzzled glance, "you're really a mystery."

He stared at her, then shook his head. "Me? I'm an open book." He filled the glass again and drained it. When it became obvious by her silence that she wasn't convinced, he sighed. "All right, I'll bite. What's so mysterious about me?"

She made a frustrated little sound deep in her throat. "You just don't add up. After seeing you here on the ranch, I can't imagine you sitting behind a desk and playing editor."

"I don't play at it," he said levelly. "I work damned hard at my job."

"And physically you're as hard as a rock. You can't tell me you got that way sitting at a desk."

"I was born and raised on a ranch." He shrugged. "I keep in shape."

"You don't talk like an editor," she burst out.

His brows shot up. "What do they talk like?" he asked with grave interest.

She gave him a harassed look. "And you don't talk like a cowboy, either."

"Does it really matter?"

Even though there was nothing but curiosity behind the question, it annoyed her. "I'm not a snob, Mac. I'm simply trying to understand you, to put a label on you."

With a speed that stunned her, he reached out, wrapped his hands around her waist, lifted her as if she weighed no more than a stick of kindling and settled her on his rock-hard thigh. "You want a label?" he murmured, touching his lips to the corner of her mouth. "Try male." He captured her lower lip, tasting, caressing with the tip of his tongue. "Try determined. Try prowling." He investigated the soft line of her throat, absorbing the light, floral fragrance that was so much a part of her. "Oh, yeah, don't forget possessive. Then toss in starved and stubborn, for good measure." The words were punctuated with small, erotic brushes of his lips against hers.

Heather's hands had a will of their own. They smoothed a sensual pattern up his chest, hesitated at his shoulders and finally met at the back of his neck.

His hands tightened around her waist. As he tugged her closer, a myriad of sensations stormed through her, making her cling to him. There was the crisp, silky warmth of his hair, the firmness of his lips, the heat of his body and the sheer, substantial strength of him that lured a woman closer, convincing her that he was a man to be trusted.

Heather stiffened. *Trusted?* The word sent an alarm pealing through her. What on earth was she doing? And with a man she'd known for such a short time! She jerked back with a lithe twist and almost succeeded in freeing herself before Mac tightened his grasp and hauled her back against him.

"Hold on, honey," he said soothingly. "Calm down."

When Heather found her voice, it was tight with alarm. Fury, she told herself, that's what it was. She definitely wasn't afraid of him. "I'm not a filly, so stop talking to me like that," she told him, trying to ease away from the heat of his body.

Mac held her right where she was.

Scowling, Heather wiggled. Heat radiated through her at the immediate and definite reaction of his body.

Mac swore. "Sweetheart," he muttered, pulling her closer, "you're going to ruin me before we even get off the ground."

"We're not going anywhere, Mackenzie, so don't worry about it," she said through gritted teeth, pushing against his chest.

He smiled lazily. "I think we are." Carefully, so he wouldn't hurt her, he removed her fists from his chest. Moments later, her arms were bound to her sides by his and she couldn't move a muscle. She shot him a look that should have shriveled his soul. It didn't. What he wanted to do was tell her that she might as well quit fighting and admit that she belonged to him. Or kiss her again. Or both.

"You couldn't be more wrong," she informed him in an arctic tone, ignoring the fact that she was still in his lap with the evidence of his aroused state pressing into her hip. "And if you think I find this macho display endearing, you've got another think coming! Let me go, Mackenzie."

"In a minute, honey."

"*Now*!"

"I want to talk to you."

"Talk? Is that what you call it? You weren't talking a minute ago."

His brows rose. "Neither were you."

Damn him. The fact that he was right did nothing to cool her temper. "That was a mistake," she admitted stiffly.

"You wanted me as much as I wanted you."

"Mackenzie," she drawled, "I learned six months ago that what I want, what I need and what's good for me could be three entirely different things."

At the deliberate provocation of her words, he slid his large hands up to her shoulders and he gave her a small shake. "We'll be good for each other," he promised.

Heather shook her head. "We're not going to have a chance to find out. I'm here to do a job. Doing it well is my primary concern. Besides, you're only going to be here a few weeks."

After dropping a swift kiss on the tip of her nose, Mac released her. His hands brushed the lush curves of her hips as she eased off his lap. Just what did she think he was going to do in these next few weeks, he wondered blankly. Sit back and watch her polish furniture?

"We'll talk about it," he promised, draping an arm around her shoulders and walking toward the front of the house.

She slanted an exasperated glance up at him. "We just *did* talk about it. It's settled."

"Umm."

Talking to him was about as effective as talking to the cottonwood tree, Heather decided huffily, her fleeting sense of satisfaction dissipating as quickly as moisture in the hot Arizona air. But it was hard to yell at a man who refused to argue, she reflected. She was thinking about that when something in his grin made her remember the cocktail parties at her parents' home, the ones with all the executive sharks, the sharks who displayed so many teeth when they smiled. And she knew why Mac's grin disturbed her. A shiver of apprehension tightened the nerves at the base of her neck just as Mac's hand on her shoulder tightened.

"What the hell is going on here?" he muttered.

Chapter Seven

Startled, she said, "Where? What's the matter?"

"That's what I'd like to know." He pointed. "Look out there."

There was the entire area between Maude's house and the barn, and at that very moment it made her think of the setting for a Broadway musical caught just at the moment before the curtain rose. Strong, geometric patterns were cast by the hot, midmorning sun. Some of the ranch hands, all clad in colorful shirts, stood in clusters, some near the walkway by Heather's house, others by the corral and barn. To a man, they lounged against whatever was available to keep them in an upright position.

"What are they all doing around here at this time of day?" Heather asked.

"Beats the hell out of me. I imagine Barney'd like the answer to that, too." Mac examined the lounging men, taking in their flamboyant finery. "Is there a rodeo in town?"

Heather shrugged. "I don't know. Why?"

"Because they're sure not dressed like that to do the haying."

"Then what . . ." Her words dwindled away as the scene before them changed. Slowly, as if the conductor of the imaginary musical had raised his baton and then swung into the opening bars, the characters began to move.

The women, who had apparently decided that they would survive—at least until they had lunch—emerged from the house, fanning out on the front porch. The cowboys, as if they were puppets pulled by the same string, came erect. And at the opposite end of the open-air stage, a door slammed. Mac and Heather turned in time to see Barney stride away from the bunkhouse and head for the corral. Even at that distance they could hear him swearing a blue streak. With just a look and a nod to discuss the issue, Heather and Mac veered in the same direction.

"I've never seen more than one or two of the men around at this time of the morning," Heather said, looking around with a puzzled frown. "So far, I've counted six. Do you suppose something's happened?"

Mac nudged his hat back thoughtfully. "I hope so, for their sake. Barney doesn't look like the milk of human kindness is running through his veins right now."

As they approached the house they heard the women exchanging laughing comments with Steve and Big John who were lingering near the walk. The two men exchanged a look, hitched up their jeans and ambled up the path toward the porch.

No, amble wasn't exactly the word for what they were doing, Heather decided. The stiff-legged, shoulder-rolling, John Wayne stride would be better described as a swagger. Or a strut. They were like two peacocks about to display their plumage to a gaggle of expectant hens.

"What's the matter with those two?" Mac muttered.

Heather wondered the same thing. At least Mac's comment proved that it wasn't her imagination. But whatever it was, it wasn't normal. And that was the strange thing, because Big John, Steve and all the others were exactly that: nice, normal men. Or they had been until today. They ordinarily wore faded, sturdy clothes that stood up to the rugged demands of ranch life, not shirts that looked like they had been dipped in fluorescent paint. And when they walked, they moved with nice, laid-back, loose-limbed strides, not like roosters measuring off their territory.

Half turning at the angry thuds of Barney's booted feet, Heather caught a glimpse of the rest of the men. Still unaware of the foreman's presence, they were sneaking glances at the women and striking elaborately casual poses at the corral fence. Whitey, a roly-poly man of middle age sucked in his stomach and approached the house.

"He looks like somebody pulled his belt in about four notches too many," Mac commented after a quick glance at the breathless man.

"Do you suppose it's some sort of a joke?" Heather asked.

Mac looked at her, his brows lifted in inquiry.

She shook her head, mystified. "I'm only guessing. A practical joke on the greenhorns, perhaps?"

"What's the point?"

"I don't know." Heather looked as baffled as she sounded. "I don't think practical jokes *have* a point."

"I don't think that's it." Mac's tone was distracted as he followed Whitey's progress. The cowboy's gut was still sucked in and his face was turning red beneath his tan. "What they're doing is more peculiar than funny. Besides, they wouldn't jeopardize Maude's new business by pulling something on her clients. Even if they were crazy enough to do it, they'd tell Barney what they were up to." He nodded, pointing out the ground-eating stride of the foreman. "He doesn't look like he's coming to join the party. For one thing, he's not dressed for it."

"That's true." Heather inspected the older man with thoughtful eyes. "You can look at him without putting on your sunglasses."

"And I get the feeling that he's coming to twist a few tail feathers."

"If the look on his face is any indication, he's going to twist a lot more than that. He's *mad*."

Mac's hand tightened fractionally on her shoulder. "I don't blame him. I would be, too, and the first one I'd jump all over is Big John."

"Why pick on him?"

"They're in the middle of haying, one of the machines is down, and instead of working on it he's over there trying to make out with the women. That enough reason?"

Make out? Heather's interest in Barney's temper and the haying dropped to zero. Make *out*? With her guests? Her *married* guests? Her gaze focused on the porch where Lou sat on the rail and laughed down at Steve and Big John. The other women were doing pretty much the same, and the men were grinning like donkeys. Yes, she supposed grimly, what they were doing could definitely be called the first stage of making out.

But, why? Or rather, why *now*? Even yesterday, a mere twenty-four hours earlier, there had been no indication that something like this was brewing. The men had gone about their business, a bit distant but polite. And last night at the corral, while Leo and Jim were convincing the women that horses didn't have homicidal tendencies, Barney would have told her if trouble was in the offing.

Heather blinked uneasily as she watched the little drama unfold in front of the house. The foreman and Whitey arrived at the same time, and with a gesture Barney drew the three men aside. He could give pointers to a corporate manager, Heather decided seconds later. He spoke so quietly his words weren't audible outside the small group, but that didn't diminish their effect. Each of the three men gave him an embarrassed grin and slid a look at the women on the porch before he took off. By that time, the others down by the corral had spotted Barney: they disappeared before he could turn his attention to them.

While the foreman gazed around, checking for strays, Heather was doing some hard thinking. She had spent most of her adult life taking measurements and working with the results, so figures held no mystery for her. And right now, she concluded uneasily, remembering the awkward conversation she'd had with Barney the night before, she was dealing with the most basic set of all: two plus two equals four. Mac's fingers flexed on her shoulder when she sighed.

If something had happened that concerned The Oasis, Barney would have told her. Of that much she was certain. Since he hadn't, she had to assume that there was nothing to tell. However, one particular part of last night's conversation—her part—had definitely caught Barney's attention, she reflected gloomily. Expecting him to remain silent was undoubtedly expecting too much—especially considering the self-satisfied smirk he'd had on his face when he'd left.

She slid a cautious glance up at Mac, only to find him watching her quizzically. Damn, damn, damn. Would she ever learn to keep her mouth shut?

Heather's groan was silent but heartfelt. Barney had probably made a beeline for the bunkhouse last night to tell the hands just how irresistible they were. The more she thought about it, the more certain she was that she was right. That would account for the peacocks that had assembled this morning, and the unexpected visits by Steve and Big John. They had obviously dressed up in their finest to give the women

a thrill. In fact, it was the only thing she could think of that *would* account for it.

"Are you okay, honey?" Mac looked down at her, inspecting her face.

Heather smiled weakly and wondered if she could get her hands around Barney's brawny neck. "I'm fine. I, uh, just remembered that I have to talk to Barney for a second. Be right back." She broke away before he could respond and sped over to Barney, who was staring at the vanishing men in disgust.

"Blabbermouth!" Scowling up at him, she added, "If this little fiasco threw your haying schedule off, it's your own fault. You deserve exactly what you got."

Barney blinked at the unexpected attack. "Hey, all I did was—"

"I know precisely what you did," she hissed, watching Mac start toward them. "You told those cowboys what I told you—"

"You didn't say it was confidential." Barney jammed his fists on his hips and met her frown with one of his own.

"Common horse sense should have told you that." Mac's curiosity was getting the best of him, she noted distractedly. He was moving closer. "Barney," she said rapidly, "I don't have time to pretty things up, so listen close. If you mention one word about sex symbols to Mac, I swear I'll personally wring your neck and feed your eyeballs to the chickens."

He grinned. "We don't have any chickens."

"I'll buy some."

Barney chuckled. "He giving you a bad time?"

"What he gives me is a lot of grief, and I don't need any more. I want your promise that you won't tell him."

He raised his hand, palm facing her. "Scout's honor."

Mac came to a halt beside Heather, eyeing the other man curiously. "Taking the pledge, Barney?"

"Yeah, reckon I am."

"What was all that about?" Mac nodded in the direction the men had taken.

Barney's gaze drifted over Heather's anxious expression. "Just a little misunderstanding. I don't think it'll happen again." Turning away he added, "But now that I've got them rounded up I'm going to make sure they get out to the field. See you later."

Heather waved at his departing back, studiously avoiding Mac's gaze.

"Are *you* going to tell me?"

She grinned at his blatant curiosity. "My lips are sealed," she said primly.

"They're more than that." His hand settled at her waist and he turned her back toward Maude's house while he waited. She wasn't going to bite, he decided. When she finally and reluctantly turned to him with raised brows, he said succinctly, "They're kissable. And tasty.

Heather stifled a sigh. "Let's not start that again."

"Are we back to your job?"

She nodded. "We are. My priorities haven't changed in the last thirty minutes."

"Hmm." He slid his hand down her arm and laced his fingers through hers. "How long would you say it takes you to restore a house?"

Stepping over a tall clump of grass, she asked, "Why?"

"Humor me, okay?"

She eyed him suspiciously. "It depends entirely upon the job."

"A ballpark figure will do."

"Two months, give or take a few problems."

"And you don't kiss anyone while you're on the job?"

"I didn't—"

"Sounds like a lot of dry spells to me." His thoughtful expression made her roll her eyes. "As you reminded me earlier, I'm only going to be here for a month and I've already used four days." He swept her along with him as he talked, one part of his mind concentrating on the growing suspicion on her face, the other on her warm body brushing against his. "Here's what I suggest. Why don't we—"

"Wait a minute." Heather dug her heels into the hard ground and yanked her hand free of his grasp. "I'm tired of being hauled from one place to another like a dog on a leash. It also sounds like you're up to something fishy, and I definitely remember telling you that I'm not interested in games." She bent over to fish a small stone from her shoe. "Exactly what is it that you want, Mackenzie?"

"You."

The stark answer rocked her right down to the soles of her sandals. She turned her head and looked up—

and wished she hadn't. He hadn't lied earlier, she realized with a sense of shock. Nor had he exaggerated. It was all there, blazing in his green eyes. He *was* prowling and possessive, a hungry male, stubborn and determined. And now he wasn't even trying to conceal it.

Tension radiated through Heather. "I don't believe I'm hearing this!" She took several agitated steps then spun around to face him. "Why me?" she demanded, throwing her arms out in a gust of pure exasperation. "I come to the middle of a desert, for God's sake, to do a simple job. All I ask is to be left alone to get on with it. Is that asking too much?" She looked upward as if waiting for an answer. When none came she supplied her own. "Apparently it is! Instead I inherit a man who's bored, who wants to play games for a month."

"At least I'm not after your money."

Infuriated by the lazy drawl and the amusement in his eyes, she jammed her hands in the back pockets of her shorts to keep from wrapping them around his throat. The movement stretched the fabric of her knit shirt tight over her breasts and his gaze didn't miss a thing. Smoldering, she said, "That was a low blow, Mackenzie."

"But it didn't hurt, did it?"

Heather could barely see him through the haze of her temper. "Hurt? You have to be kidding."

"And I'll bet it didn't hurt when your ex-fiancé tipped his hand."

"I was madder than hell."

"Ah."

The complacency in his voice was more maddening than the amusement, she decided. "Don't 'ah' me. I walked away from him without a backward glance."

"Bright girl."

"And don't patronize me. I'm a woman."

"I know."

Heather groaned aloud at the sexy masculine growl of appreciation. Would she ever learn? Now they were right back where they had started, with his eyes eating her up and making promises that sent shivers down her spine. "Now don't start that again," she said hastily. "You've made your point."

"Which one is that?" he asked mildly.

She took a deep breath and exhaled slowly. It didn't help. "You really are a maddening man." Her eyes narrowing at his sudden grin, she said clearly and concisely, "I am going back to work now and I don't want to play any more games. I want to be left alone. Undisturbed. Is that quite clear?"

"Quite." He cupped her chin with his hard fingers and swiftly dipped his head, brushing her lips with his. "But, you can't stay in that house for a whole month, honey. I'll be waiting."

Heather sat on the porch swing as the sun crested the Santa Catalina Mountains. Watching the hot, golden sphere bring color and life in its wake was a daily ritual that never failed to fascinate her. All in all, she reflected, it was the best time of the day. The guests were still in bed, the morning air had a bite, she had a cup of perfectly brewed coffee beside her and there was plenty of time to think.

It was amazing how quickly four days had passed, she reflected with a sigh of satisfaction. Four days of relative peace and quiet. The ranch hands were practically back to normal, at least in respect to their clothing. There was still a residual knee-jerk reaction of sucked in bellies and tightened buns when they were around any of the guests. And the women had lost all signs of restlessness, settling in with an ease that amazed her. They swam, they disappeared for hours on the horses, they entertained themselves in the evenings and best of all they weren't drooling over Millie's daily menus—at least not when she was around. There was even an occasional air of suppressed excitement about them which she had chalked up to the accomplishment of their latest goals—whatever they might be.

The business was working, far more easily than she'd expected. In fact she had so much time to herself she had read the Sunday magazines the day they'd arrived. The fact that the newspaper had sent them overnight mail seemed to indicate that they were eager to hear from her, she reflected optimistically. The first time she'd scanned them, moving rapidly from one article to the next. The second and third readings had been more thorough, done with rising excitement. That evening she had plugged in her typewriter and completed a rough draft. Since then, she had rewritten it several times. How much work it still needed, she would learn as soon as she gathered the nerve to hand it to Mac.

Mac. If there was a fly in the ointment, it was Mac. He had perfected an approach that kept her on edge but stopped short of pushing her into an all-out retreat. She knew exactly what he was doing and it *still* drove her crazy. He dropped in when she least expected him, just long enough to remind her that he was around. He would prowl around, taking in her every breath and gesture with those damned devil eyes until she was ready to scream, then disappear.

Sighing, Heather put down her mug and stepped away from the swing. Someday, she promised herself as she walked across the yard, she'd pay him back. She didn't know how or when, but she would. Coming to a halt by a scarlet bougainvillea that was running rampant at one corner of the split-rail fence, she stooped down to pick up some dead leaves at the base of the plant.

She was on her hands and knees, scooping the leaves to one side, when a cheerful whistle started near the corral and moved in her direction. She looked up, saw Big John and sat back on her heels. It wasn't until she raised her hand in greeting that she realized he couldn't see her behind the dense bush. Before she could call out, he waved and yelled to someone further down the walk.

"Hey, Steve."

"Yo, B.J."

The two men met near the bougainvillea and Heather rose to her knees.

"Well, did one of them corner you this morning?"

"Yeah, the little one with the dark hair."

Heather sank back down.

"Third day in a row for me."

"Me, too."

Big John heaved a sigh. "Swear to God, Steve, I don't know how much longer I can hold out. It was the tall blonde this morning. God, does that woman have a mouth on her. She gets to talking and pretty soon I don't even know what day it is."

Heather gasped and covered her mouth with her hand. Lou?

"Yeah, I know. She was after me yesterday before the sun was even up."

Lou?

"I wonder if they're climbing all over the other guys like this."

"I don't know for sure, but I'd say at least a couple. Some of 'em are getting mighty edgy."

"Yeah, I noticed."

"I'll tell you, B.J., my mama didn't raise no saint. One of these days real soon I'm just going to say to hell with the whole thing and tell 'em yes."

"Tell which one?"

"Whichever one's doing the offering that day."

"It's mighty tempting."

"And the stakes are getting higher all the time."

"Barney would kill us," B.J. said morosely.

"Yeah. He'd have to stand in line, though. Heather and Maude would be there first, with Mac right behind them."

"Suppose we could put in for hazardous-duty pay?"

"I'm thinking about it. Jeez, B.J., this used to be an easy job."

"Yeah. One week and five women make a big difference. I think I'd rather get kicked by a horse once in a while than run the gauntlet every day with these females."

"How much longer are they gonna be here?"

"Barney said this first bunch is staying two weeks."

"Oh, God. That means another full week?"

"You got it."

Steve swore softly. "I'll tell you straight, B.J., the way they're dangling all that stuff in front of my nose, I'll be lucky to last another day."

Stuff? Heather blinked. Exactly what *stuff* were they dangling?

Big John cleared his throat. "You gonna be gone all day again?"

"Yeah, I'm just waiting for Millie to get the lunches ready."

"Me, too. I'm heading out in the other direc—"

"Heather? Yoo-hoo, Heather!" Lou's call came from inside the house.

"Oh, hell. There's that blonde again. I'm gone."

"Not without me, you aren't."

Heather stared dejectedly at the brilliant cascade of blooms in front of her. She didn't believe it. None of the women was the type to chase and deliberately seduce a ranch hand. They were decent. And married. With *children*, for heaven's sake! Of course, they did have too much money at their disposal and too much time on their hands, she acknowledged glumly. Their husbands were on extended trips for their various companies and their kids were at summer camp.

She shook her head. Even so, these weren't jaded women out for cheap thrills. She'd bet her life and what little fortune she had on that. Heather picked up the brown leaves she'd brushed together and reconsidered. Maybe not her life, she decided. And maybe just ten dollars. Or five.

The two men were fast on their feet, she had to give them that. There wasn't a trace of them when Lou stuck her head out the door and said, "There you are. We wondered if you wanted to join us. We're going riding."

Heather winced and wondered wretchedly if she was going to be looking for hidden meanings whenever one of the women spoke to her. She got to her feet slowly, lifting her hand in acknowledgment. Forcing her voice to sound natural, she said, "Thanks, but I think I'll pass. You go on. Oh," she added hastily, waving toward the north, "be sure to take the usual trail. The men said they saw a bunch of, uh . . . skunks the other way."

Lou flashed a smile. "Right. Sure you don't want to go?" When Heather shook her head, she shrugged. "Okay. By the way, you just got a person-to-person call, but when I couldn't find you the man told the operator he'd try later. He had a *very* interesting voice."

When Heather's heart jumped, she was reminded that some things in life take longer than six months to forget. It was not her ex-fiancé, she told herself sternly. Even a no-class lout like Jerrold would think twice before trying to work his way back into her life. But then, maybe he *had* thought twice. "Was it collect?"

"Nope."

Heather smiled. That took care of Jerrold. "I guess I'll just have to wait."

Lou looked down the walk past Heather. "Not alone, you won't. Here comes Mac."

"Oh, God."

Laughing, Lou said heartlessly. "This time you can't use us for cover. We're taking off. See you."

Heather dashed for the house. She'd give him the article, she decided. And a nice big red pencil. That should keep him occupied for awhile.

Chapter Eight

Heather sat next to him on the couch, her gaze never leaving his expressionless face.

Mac turned the pages silently. When he finally looked up, she was chewing her fingernail and asking a silent question with her eyes. "You're not going to tell me this is a rough draft, are you?" he demanded.

"Of course not," Heather said indignantly. "I've worn off my fingerprints retyping the darn thing. How is it?"

"How many rewrites did you do?"

"I don't know, I lost count." Impatience snapping in her dark eyes, she asked, "Well, is it any good?"

"What do you think?"

"Mac! Do you have to keep answering my questions with more questions?" She leaned back on the sofa and sighed noisily. "If I'd known what to think,

I wouldn't have given it to you. You're the expert here, not me."

He turned back to the first page. "Why did you start with the house completed?"

"I'm not sure." Heather nervously eyed the red pencil he was tapping against his knee. "It just seemed more interesting that way. Mac, if you're going to do major surgery on it, would you get started? I can't stand the suspense."

"Okay." He gathered the pages and tidily lined up the edges.

"Wait!" Her hand touched his thigh. "Maybe you could just, uh, tell me what needs to be done."

He brushed a finger over her slim hand in a fleeting caress. "I can show you quicker."

Heather went to work on her second nail. When his fingers tightened around the pencil, she burst out, "Could you just give me a bottom-line evaluation before you start mutilating it? You know, a succinct appraisal—like good, bad or indifferent?"

Mac sighed. "It's good."

She brightened. "You wouldn't like to expand on that a bit, would you? I mean, it'd be nice to know if that means so-so, a really solid good, or what-we-have-here-is-a-Pulitzer-Prize-winner-in-the-wings." She had a sudden attack of paranoia. "Or is 'good' what you tell people when you can't think of anything else to say?"

She looked so rattled, he couldn't help it. He leaned over and kissed her on the tip of her nose. "It's *good*. Now stop interrupting."

Heather couldn't watch. Instead she closed her eyes and agonized over the sound of the pencil slashing over the paper. She took a deep breath and told herself firmly to relax. When that didn't work, she deliberately turned her attention to her guests. It might be true that she was idealistic—too idealistic according to her brother—and wanted to believe the best about people, but something just didn't ring true. Lou and the others were *nice*. She just couldn't believe they would cold-bloodedly set about seducing veritable strangers.

When Mac turned another page, her concentration broke. At the rate she was going she wouldn't have a decent nail left, she thought in disgust. Writing was the easy part, she decided a moment later. Carefully selecting a word which she'd later discard as totally inappropriate had been an agonizing process, but it was nothing compared to the refined torture of sitting next to a power-mad editor with a red pencil in his hand. Was she masochistic, after all? Did she have some previously undetected, deep-seated desire to suffer? Did she—

"Okay, you can look now."

Heather's eyes snapped open and she stared down at the trail of red squiggles, appalled. "What have you done to my baby?"

"Tightened it up," he said heartlessly. "You toss adjectives around as if they're rose petals."

"God meant writers to use adjectives," she said stoutly. "Otherwise he would have made skinnier dictionaries."

Mac turned to face her, his gaze resting on her mutinous expression. "Poor baby. Do you want to stomp around the room for a few minutes? Throw a couple of vases?"

Heather glared, intensely annoyed by his provoking grin. "Stuff it, Mackenzie. Let's make your day— tell me the worst."

Dropping a hand to her slim shoulder, he said cheerfully, "There is no worst. It's good."

"Good?" Outrage gleaming in her brown eyes, she demanded, "Well, why didn't you tell me that in the first place?"

"I did. You didn't believe me."

"I thought you were being kind," she grumbled.

"Editors are never that kind," he informed her calmly. "If I say it's good, it's good. The time to start worrying is when I say it shows promise. Now, let's get to work."

In the next hour, Heather revised her opinion of editors in general and Mac in particular. "I take it back," she told him expansively.

"Take what back?"

"What I was thinking about you earlier."

He leaned closer, pressing his shoulder against hers. "As a man or an editor?"

She ignored both the pressure and the question. "I thought you'd come at this with a chain saw rather than a pencil. In fact," she said generously, "you did a great job. At times, I sound absolutely brilliant."

"At times," he retorted, "you *are* brilliant."

Heather blinked up at him. "Really?"

Mac sighed. "Yes," he said succinctly. "I mean it. Positively. Absolutely. I'm not joking. You're good. Very good. In fact if you were looking for a job I'd consider hiring you."

"Oh." It was a breathless, surprised sound. Then Heather chuckled, recovering fast. "I'm overwhelmed. Stunned. Astonished. Dumbfounded. Flabbergasted. Also appreciative. But if you paid by the piece I'd starve." She tapped the pages with a slim finger. "Do you know how much time I spent on this?"

"It was worth it," he said briefly. "It's a great piece for your first article."

"First?" Her brows rose. "It's the one and only."

"You'll be asked for more," he said with certainty. "And you should definitely agree to do them. I'm serious, honey. You could put articles like this to work for you. They could turn your career in a whole new direction, give you options you've never even thought of."

Heather tilted her head thoughtfully, examining his face. She made a noncommittal little sound and sorted absently through the last couple of pages. "Hey!" She stared at the solid red line running through every single sentence of the last two paragraphs. "You took away my ending."

He smiled at her affronted expression. "So I did."

"I may not be an editor, but even I know I can't send it in that way."

"Correct. You write a new one."

"Why? That was a perfectly good—"

He held up his hand to stop the indignant spate of words. "It was," he agreed, "but not for this. Look, the thrust of this article was reconverting an old house into a business, right?" He waited for her reluctant nod. "At the end, you're pouring in a lot of information about running the business. What you need to do is circle back to your beginning. Discuss the finishing touches, compare the before and after, deal with any part of it you like as long as you stay on the subject."

"But—"

"And these," he tapped the deleted paragraphs with his pencil, "are a perfect lead-in for a second article." He grinned at the sudden gleam in her eyes. "When you send in the finished copy, tell the editor some of the experience you've had with running the business end of things and see if he's interested."

"Aside from your talent as a teacher, you're a genius." Heather looked at the last page with narrowed eyes. "You're also right, and I know exactly how I'll fix it."

"Fine." He handed her the pencil. "Don't tell me, show me."

Heather was putting the manuscript in a drawer of the desk when the telephone shrilled at her elbow. She caught it on the second ring. "Good morning, The Oasis, Heather speaking."

A deep, impatient masculine voice said, "Good. I was afraid you'd be out herding cattle or something. How are you, Sis?"

"Oh, hi, Les."

Something in her voice brought Mac's head up. His green eyes narrowed and locked on her expressive face.

"Is this the monthly checkup call? If so, I'm fine," she told him cheerfully, wondering if his antennae were working overtime, if he had somehow conjured up Mac's presence at the ranch. Telling herself she was getting paranoid, she chuckled. "Business is booming, and so far they haven't made me milk cows or cut hay. Are you at home?"

"Nope, California. Otherwise I'd have been down to see you."

Heather closed her eyes, grateful for whatever land deal had taken him out of town. The last thing she needed was Les doing his big-brother routine, running credit checks on every male within a ten-mile radius. "I got a card from the folks today. They're in Greece."

"Yeah, I heard, too. Sounds like they're having a good time." His tone changed. "But I want to know about you. You can't work *all* the time. Are you...enjoying yourself?"

Oh, Lord. Heather stifled a groan. Translated, that meant was she seeing anyone? If so, would she please supply his name, Social Security number, driver's license and a list of his credit cards. If possible, please also send banking and personal references.

"I'm having a wonderful time," she said chattily. "I've actually had some spare time and I'm trying my hand at writing."

There was a silence at the other end of the line. "Writing?" Les asked cautiously.

Heather grinned. It wasn't often that she was able to divert him, and she took a great deal of pleasure in her few successes. "Writing," she repeated with deep satisfaction.

"How'd that come about?" He still sounded disconcerted.

"Believe it or not, a local newspaper asked me to write an article about this house for their Sunday supplement."

"I hate to sound negative, Sis, but what the hell do you know about writing?"

"Actually," she admitted, absently smoothing a thumb over her braid, "that was my first reaction, too. But Mac reminded me that I had the expertise and convinced me to try."

"Mac?" His tone registered such a blend of suspicion and satisfaction that she wouldn't have been surprised if he'd shouted *"ah hah, a man!"* "Who's Mac?" he asked neutrally.

Heather swore softly and cast a look of frustrated apology at Mac. He grinned and mouthed *big brother?* When she nodded he leaned back and crossed his arms over his chest, apparently willing to be entertained.

"Mac is Maude's nephew," she told him grouchily.

"Maude being the lady you met in the gym?"

"You know damn well who Maude is. Don't be difficult."

"And does Mac have a last name?"

Heather grimly reminded herself that Les was her brother and annoying as he was she still loved him— even if he did have an overdeveloped sense of responsibility where she was concerned, especially since her parents weren't around to fend off the wolves he imagined were always nipping at her heels.

She turned her back on Mac and said sharply, "His name is Wade Mackenzie, but you can relax, brother dear. He's not my lover, nor will he be."

When he finally spoke, her brother's voice was gentle. "I'm sorry, babe. I know you're a big girl, but I hate to see you hurt."

"Les—"

"And as much as it goes against the grain, I'd rather see you with a lover than another phony fiancé."

"I told you—"

"Look, Sis," he said hurriedly, "I've got to go. I'll drop in and see you when I'm in the area. 'Bye."

"I don't believe that man," she muttered in disgust, replacing the receiver, aware that sooner or later she'd have to turn around and face the music.

"He's worried about you." Mac's hand fell on her shoulder and she jumped. "Don't be so hard on him."

Heather eased away, putting the desk between them before she met his gaze. "I hope you're still as understanding when you realize that he's going to run a check on you," she retorted. "Probably one that goes all the way back to kindergarten."

He shrugged. "I'd do the same for my sister."

Diverted, she said, "Do you have one?"

"Two. But there's something else I'd like to discuss with you if—"

"Older or younger?"

"Younger, both of them," he said impatiently.

"And do you play the heavy big brother?"

"I have on occasion. Not lately, though. They're both married happily with children. Now if we could just get back to—"

"I'm sorry about Les," Heather blurted, acknowledging that she wasn't going to keep him off the embarrassing subject of her brother. When sheer persistence was the issue, she reflected dryly, the two men had a great deal in common.

He waved his hand as if he were flicking away an annoying gnat. "Your brother doesn't bother me. Something you said, though—"

Suddenly realizing what the problem was, Heather interrupted him again. "I'm sorry I brought up your name. Truly. I should have known better. Actually," she amended, "I *do* know better. I thought my writing would be a perfect ploy, but as usual my tongue ran away with—"

Mac broke in ruthlessly. "I don't give a damn what he knows about me."

"Then what—"

"You told him I wasn't your lover."

"Of course I did," she said righteously. "You're not."

"You also said that I never would be."

"Well?" She eyed him doubtfully for a moment, then drew herself up to her full sixty-five inches, everyone of them bristling with defiance. "I simply told the truth."

His crooked smile accepted the challenge. "Don't write me off yet, honey."

Deciding that provoking Mac wasn't the wisest thing to do, especially since she didn't seem to have the backbone of an eel when he turned those sea-green eyes on her, Heather backpedaled as fast as she could. "Speaking of writing," she said lightly, "when do you think I should send in my article?"

"As soon as you make those changes and tack on a new ending." Mac shoved his hands in his back pockets and rocked back on his heels, aware of the anxiety buried beneath her lightness.

That was a definite sign of progress, he decided with a rush of primitive masculine satisfaction. The wary, "can you be trusted?" glances aimed at him earlier simply because he had been a male, had been replaced by ones that said "you make me very, very nervous." The message, as clear as if it had been spoken aloud, was meant only for him. And that was exactly the way he wanted it. He had observed the comfortable camaraderie with which she treated the other men and approved of it wholeheartedly. It was fine. For them. But for now, he'd rather have her on edge around him. He didn't want her treating him like a brother. He was a man bent on breaking through that protective barrier she'd erected around herself, and he wanted her aware of the fact, aware of him, every minute of the day and night.

"Tomorrow," she decided, moving restlessly away from the desk and the look on his face. "I'll get to it first thing."

"Well," Lou asked, "have you had any luck with Steve?"

Gini shook her head. "No more than you have with Whitey."

Jill spoke up. "I tried that new guy, Adam, and he was just as tough as the rest of them."

"I never thought they'd last this long," Susan said gloomily.

Heather stopped in midstride, grateful that she hadn't used a flashlight to illuminate the darkness. She had spent the last hour at the pool, swimming away her tension, and now, clad in no more than sandals and her suit, she held her breath and listened. The five women were just around the corner on the back porch, in the hot tub.

If she had any scruples, she reflected, she'd step out and let them know they had an audience. Fortunately, at least at the present moment, she didn't. At a time like this she couldn't afford such niceties. Her business was at stake. She leaned against the house and waited.

It wasn't long before Chris asked plaintively, "Do we give up?"

"Bite your tongue," Gini told her.

"We have just begun to fight," Susan said dramatically.

Jill, the practical one, mused, "It's all a matter of finding the right button to push."

"I haven't met my goal yet," Lou stated in a calm voice.

Goal? Heather froze. Good God, what *was* her goal? To seduce the entire staff?

"Has anyone lost any weight?" Jill asked.

The uproarious laughter made the hair on the back of Heather's neck stand on end.

Gini's voice finally broke through the snickering. "Once we found the bakery, did anyone seriously expect to?"

"Not me," four voices chorused.

"Well, I think we should have," Jill muttered. "When you consider how many miles we had to ride north before we could angle around and head south, we surely burned something up."

"We did," Gini stated firmly. "The seat of our pants. But it was worth it. After several days of cold-turkey abstinence, I would have *walked* it."

"And just think," Lou murmured, "it all came about because of Jill's skepticism."

"Long live our little pragmatist," Gini said.

Crystal clinked as the women voiced their approval.

Jill's amused voice broke through. "Well I ask you, were we really expected to buy the 'bobcat' routine?"

"Don't forget the kangaroo rats."

"And the rattlers."

"Well, we can't say they didn't try," Lou observed fairly. "Barney certainly had Leo and Jim trained. After the first day when Leo took us out, one of them always rode a little way with us just to make sure we knew which direction was north."

"And God knows Heather tried hard enough," Gini stated. "I found it rather endearing, the way she mother-henned us, always waving us off toward the foothills."

Somehow, Heather wasn't surprised. With perfect hindsight, she recalled their general air of self-satisfaction. In fact, she mused, if she used their change of attitude as a guide, she could probably pin-point the exact day they had struck gold—or choco-late. She pressed her shoulders more comfortably against the house and waited for reaction to set in. The Oasis was ruined before it got off the ground. It hadn't even survived ten days.

"You're right," Chris agreed. "Everyone here did their best to cover up, but I think that the lion's share of credit goes to Heather. Maude, dear little dump-ling that she is, couldn't have masterminded such a scheme."

Susan spoke up. "Just as a matter of curiosity, I wonder when Heather learned about the bakery. She certainly couldn't have known when she opened the place."

"It must have been quite a shock."

That could be classified as the understatement of the year, Heather mused as she eased into the darker shadow of a cottonwood where she could see the women.

Lou cleared her throat. "Ladies, we have a deci-sion to make before we leave."

Shaking her head, Gini said, "We still have plenty of time and I move that we don't get serious before we have to."

"We at least have to think about it." Lou lifted a bottle of mineral water and topped off the glasses. "Has any of you seen the reservation book for next week? Anyone know who's going to be here?"

Susan raised her glass. "I saw it. There are just four, all from the gym."

"Who are they?"

"Doris Managar, Elsie, Joan Trevor and Mindy Scofield."

Gini broke the lengthy silence. "Poor Heather."

"Well," Lou said briskly, "that settles it as far as I'm concerned."

"Settles what?" The other four looked at her blankly.

"The question I was about to pose. We have a decision to make, but before we can make it we have to consider the people who are following us. Elsie, Joan and Mindy aren't so bad, but Doris is sour enough to spoil the week for everyone. Is everyone agreed?"

They all nodded.

"So?" Susan finally asked. "Where does that leave us?"

Lou took a swallow of water. "Deciding whether or not we're going to let the next batch of guests reap the benefits of all our hard work."

"What do you mean?"

Lou's smile was nothing short of Machiavellian. "Do we tell them about the bakery?"

Awed, Jill said, "That is absolutely wicked."

Lou nodded complacently. "I know."

"I love it!" Chris grinned and leaned back, a beatific expression covering her face.

"You mean," Gini said, "we tell them nothing? At all?"

Lou cleared her throat. "I rather fancy the idea of dropping a hint or two."

"How big, or should I say how small of a hint?" Susan waited, laughter gleaming in her eyes.

"It's quite simple. And very polite. We'll get home the evening before they leave and I suggest that we give them a courtesy call. Tell them how much we enjoyed ourselves and wish them a wonderful week. Then we can just casually mention that we found a treasure trove of goodies."

"And when they ask where it is?"

"We tell them that a big part of the fun is finding it, and we're certainly not going to deprive them of that particular joy. We assure them that if they look hard enough and are persistent enough they'll find it."

Heather could hardly believe it. She watched the grinning women, satisfaction practically oozing from their pores, while she considered the ramifications of their little plot. It meant that The Oasis had a fighting chance. It wouldn't automatically go out of business when the first batch of guests left. It could even start a new trend: a fat farm with a built-in bakery— if one could find it.

"I think we should give them one more bit of information," Jill said seriously.

"What's that?"

Her grin broke out, ruining the somber effect. "I think we should sort of accidentally tell them that the cowboys know where it is but that they're sworn to secrecy."

Gini snickered, breaking the appreciative silence. "That's really dirty. They'll drive those guys nuts."

"I know." Jill's voice was dreamy with satisfaction.

Even Heather, tucked securely behind the leafy cottonwood, had to laugh. There was undoubtedly

something lacking in her executive outlook, she reflected, but she found the whole thing very entertaining.

Chris said thoughtfully, "As a bonus, when we
leave, just so Heather can tighten security, I suggest
that we tell what tipped us off to the existence of the
bakery. After all, if we found one of Bertha's bags out
by the trees, so could the next batch of guests."

Jill agreed. "Yeah, if it had been old and battered
we wouldn't have thought a thing about it, but it was
a dead giveaway when we found fresh brownie crumbs
and a smear of fresh fudge frosting in it. But I don't
know why we should tell Heather."

"How easy do we want to make it on the next
group?" Chris retorted.

"You've got a point. We'll let her know so she can
warn the hands. Everybody agree?"

The informal vote was unanimous.

"One last thing," Lou pointed out. "About the
other thing. Do we continue our campaign with the
men?"

The others nodded.

"Good. I think some of them are near the breaking
point. I was wondering if we'd have a better chance if
we followed them on horseback. Maybe if we each got
one of them alone we'd have better luck."

Gini raised a finger. "Question. If one of us does
succeed, do we share?"

Lou shook her head and folded her arms across her
chest for emphasis. "Absolutely not. This is definitely a case of every woman for herself!"

Chapter Nine

Every woman for herself.

The words haunted Heather. As each day passed, she agreed more heartily with the aphorism that ignorance was bliss. She would've liked a bit of that bliss, she thought darkly, watching Steve's head appear around the corner of the barn. Nothing moved except his eyeballs, which rolled from side to side inspecting the corral. When he was apparently convinced that no terrors lurked in the area, his neck and shoulders appeared, immediately followed by the rest of him. Stealthily he tiptoed through the corral leading his saddled horse.

That morning as well as the past three mornings Heather had risen while it was still dark, hoping to discover at least one of the women in the midst of a...transaction. She had heard Steve and Big John talk about it, she had heard the women themselves discussing it, but Heather knew that she would only believe it if she witnessed it herself.

Of course, she confessed silently, what she hoped to find was that the whole thing was a misunderstanding, that somehow she had misinterpreted what she'd overheard. But she had a dismal feeling that was not about to happen. With a shrug she acknowledged grimly that bliss and ignorance would do nothing to prepare her when the time for action arrived. Sooner or later she would have to handle the situation and then only the truth would serve her.

With that gloomy thought to cheer her, she stepped from behind a clump of acacia. "'Morning, Steve."

"Agh!" Steve jumped, startling his horse. When they had both settled down, he took off his hat and wiped his brow with his sleeve. "Damn, Heather, you scared the living . . . daylights out of me."

"Sorry. I wasn't thinking." She looked at the pack behind his saddle. "Are you going to be out all day?"

"Yeah." The glance he threw over his shoulder was a quick, nervous reflex. "Uh, Heather, do you think you could keep your voice down a little?"

Her brows drew together in a surprised frown. "Sure," she whispered. "Why?"

"I, uh, just don't want to wake anybody up," he muttered, peeking over his other shoulder.

Well, that answer was as good as any she was going to get, she thought dryly, glancing back at her house, which was roughly two hundred yards distant yet still the closest one around. "Who else is going out with you?" she said softly.

"B.J., Whitey and a couple of the new guys." He jerked a thumb over his shoulder. "We'll be out at the far end haying."

"Why Big John?" she asked in surprise. "I thought he always worked around here."

"Not during haying season." He shifted restlessly and took another look around. "Barney likes to keep him near the machinery."

"Oh."

"Hey, listen, Heather," Steve said urgently. "I'd like to talk but I've got to get going."

"Oh, sure. Sorry." She sighed enviously as he flowed into the saddle with a lithe movement and urged his horse down the path. She watched until he disappeared into the darkness, then—still not sure what she expected to find—Heather turned and headed for the barn.

"What are you doing out here so early?"

Heather gasped at the soft question, whirling around just as Mac stepped beside her. "Do you have to sneak around like Natty Bumppo? You scared me half to death!"

"It seems to be contagious," he commented, draping his arm across her shoulders. "I saw Steve leap like a wounded deer when you stepped out of the bushes." He looked down at her. "Is it my imagination or are the men just a tad jumpy these days?"

Gazing up at him wide-eyed, she said, "Whatever makes you say that?"

"Well, for starters, they're not strutting around posing anymore. As a matter of fact," he said thoughtfully, ''they fall all over themselves trying to get away when the women walk up to them.''

"Umm, now that you mention it, I guess I have noticed.'' Yes, indeedy, she certainly had.

Mac cupped her shoulder in his hand, squeezing gently. ''You wouldn't have any notion of what's going on, would you?''

"Me?'' Lying through her teeth, she said calmly, ''I haven't the foggiest idea.''

"I've known these guys for a long time and I've never seen them like this.''

"Maybe they're shy.''

"Sure.''

As they reached the corner of the barn and stopped by a pile of hay, Heather's smile died as suddenly as it had dawned. Even in the dim light, she could see that B.J. had his horse out in front and he was moving fast. With short, choppy movements he tied a bundle behind his saddle, strapping it down securely. As he worked, he glanced around, his agitation evident in the set of his shoulders.

"Barney must have given him an earful the other day,'' Mac murmured. ''I don't think I've ever seen him move so fast.'' His last word ended in a grunt when Heather dug her elbow in his ribs.

"Hush. I don't want him to know we're here!''

He rubbed his ribs absently and looked down at her profile. "Why?''

"Shh!'' Heather stiffened, narrowing her eyes as a dark patch moved closer to the man and horse.

"'Morning, Big John.''

Lou's soft contralto was a breathy whisper, the words a lilting seduction.

"Well, hell!" B.J.'s rumble was not an appreciative sound.

Mac grew rigid at Heather's side. "I'll be damned," he murmured, looking down just in time to catch the expression of stoic resignation on her face. His hand slid down to her waist and he tugged her closer. "Hey, you look like you've just lost your last friend."

"My illusions," she said briefly, "which is almost as bad."

"They're consenting adults," he reminded her, watching the tall blonde run her hand down B.J.'s brawny arm.

"That doesn't make it any easier."

"I got up extra early just so I could see you, B.J.," Lou purred.

B.J. pulled the strap taut and grunted. "Lou, if I told you once, I told you a hundred times, I *like* working here. Maude's a fine boss, and I'm not gonna do anything that would upset her."

Lou's fingers walked their way back up his arm. "I do so like a man with scruples."

"I don't know why," he muttered, jerking his arm away. "It just means that you aren't gonna get what you want."

"No, no, no," she soothed, following him around to the other side of the horse. "It just makes the getting all the sweeter when it happens."

Heather groaned. She couldn't believe what she was seeing, and seeing all too clearly as the black sky became a gunmetal gray that was growing lighter with each passing second. Big John ducked his head, deliberately bumping his forehead against the saddle several times, apparently hoping the jarring action would result in a way out of his dilemma.

"Now, B.J.," Lou murmured with sweet reason, "we've been all through this before." She ran a gentle hand over the white-knuckled fist he had locked on the saddle horn. "All you have to do is say yes. Just once, and I'll quit bothering you."

Once? Heather nibbled on her mangled fingernail. All she wanted was *once*? The blasted woman wasn't even trying to pretend that her feelings were involved.

Mac leaned down until his lips touched Heather's ear. "I'm getting out of here. Voyeurism isn't exactly my bag. Coming?"

Heather shook her head, her eyes fixed on the two near the horse, standing on tiptoe so she could see over the wisps of hay. "No. When I talk to her, I want to be sure I know what I'm talking about."

"Do you have any doubts?" he asked in amazement. "She isn't mincing any words."

"I'm staying," she said stubbornly. "Go if you want to, but for heaven's sake be quiet!"

Mac heaved a disgusted sigh and muttered something about obstinate women, but he stayed right next to her.

"Not once, not twice, not ever," Big John said with a stolid resistance that astonished Heather. "Word would get around and then I'd have all the other women crawling out of the woodwork, ambushing me, wanting the same thing."

NEVER ON SUNDAE   153

Heather blinked. Well the man might have scruples, but he certainly wasn't modest!

Mac leaned closer. "I think he's let this sex-symbol talk go to his head."

Heather whirled to face him. One look told her all she needed to know. "I'm going to strangle Barney," she said calmly.

Mac's grin was provoking. He put his hand over her mouth, saying, "Shh. Barney didn't tell me."

Peeling his fingers away, one by one, Heather finally managed, "Then how did you find out?"

"Honey, did you honestly think that with every cowboy on the place preening and strutting around, that I *wouldn't* find out?"

"John," Lou's honeyed tone didn't completely cover a tinge of exasperation, "it's not as if you'd be giving me something that couldn't be replaced. There's always more available."

Heather's eyes widened. "I don't believe that woman! Doesn't she have any shame?" When she turned to face the couple Mac's arms slid around her waist, his hands settled gently on her stomach, pressing her back against him.

"Of course," he rumbled softly in her ear, "I didn't know if *I* was included in the sex-symbol category, seeing that I'm only a part-time cowboy."

With her back turned to him, Heather felt safe enough to grin. He really was an impossible man. "Don't push it, Mackenzie," she warned.

Big John reared back and took a good look at his tormentor. "What's mine is mine," he stated with flinty obstinacy, moving away from Lou's caressing fingertips. "It don't matter whether or not it can be replaced."

"Good for you, John," Heather whispered. She had always been a sucker for the underdog, and in the present situation she had a strong feeling that John was outclassed. "Hang in there, guy."

"Of course," Mac added, nuzzling her ear, "some people think that editors are sexy."

"John, dear," Lou cooed, "every time we've talked the ante has gone up. You know how high the stakes are now, don't you?"

For a moment, B.J. visibly weakened. Then with a shake of his head, he rallied. "Nope, my mind's made up. I won't do it. I won't take the risk of upsetting Maude."

Heather looked over her shoulder at Mac. "I didn't know Maude was so straitlaced."

He tilted his head and dropped a kiss on her soft lips. "I didn't, either."

"How can it bother Maude," Lou asked reasonably, "if she never finds out?" A flurry of movement distracted her, and when she got a good look she muttered, "Oh, drat!"

Any other time Mac's kiss would have kept her glued to him, but at Lou's disgusted tone Heather stepped back and craned her neck. Jill moved forward, eyeing the two by the horse.

"John," she breathed, "after all we've been through, how could you even consider—"

Throwing up his hands in disgust, he said, "Now don't carry on so. I'm not considering anything. With anybody. Not you, not her, not nobody."

Jill turned her attention to Lou. "And you, my friend," she said softly, "are poaching."

Mac whistled softly. "What is *with* this guy? He's got those women crawling all over him, practically begging, and he doesn't give an inch."

"Shh!"

Lou and Jill turned at the sound of footsteps. "For heaven's sake," Lou exclaimed to no one in particular, "are they *all* coming for B.J. this morning?"

Maude came around the far corner of the barn, her face brightening when she saw the three of them. "Ah, B.J., just the man I wanted to see. Good morning, Lou, Jill, are you visiting John?" While the two women exchanged a meaningful glance, she murmured, "How nice. We can never have too many friends."

B.J. was not a man to miss an opportunity, and with Maude's arrival he obviously saw freedom in the offing. He moved around the horse, ready to make a quick getaway, when Maude stopped him. Quite innocently she leaned against his saddle and looked up at him with a smile.

"I know you're very busy now, B.J., but would you look at my ceiling fan when you have a chance? It's making a strange grinding noise, but it doesn't move."

"Sure thing," he promised with a resigned nod. "But in the meantime don't turn it on. Okay?"

"Okay." Maude gave the horse a pat and with a smile for Lou and Jill, she bustled away.

The two women waited until she was out of sight, then turned to John. "All right, B.J.," Jill said, "this is the moment of truth. All cards on the table. Last

bet. You know where our cars are stored in town." She
dug in her oversize purse and eventually pulled out a
key ring. "I have in my hot little fist the keys to my
new Mercedes. It's yours for a night on the town if you
say yes."

"I don't believe this," Mac muttered in astonishment.

"Let's not be too hasty," Lou said, walking over to
a wooden bench and upending the tote bag she'd
brought with her. Digging into the collection of cos-
metics and basic necessities, she extracted two items.
Moving closer to B.J. and ignoring Jill, she jangled a
set of car keys. "This represents a candy-apple-red
Corvette," she tempted. "Brand new. Loaded. And
this," she held up a small, rectangular piece of plastic, "is my charge card. Both are yours for a night. No
questions asked."

"Hey, no fair," Jill protested. "I have a card, too."
She rummaged through her bag. "I know it's in here
somewhere."

Lou's smile was the equivalent of a cat licking cream
off its whiskers. "You set the rules, my friend. You
said it was the last bet. Mine just happens to be higher
than yours."

With a muttered oath, Big John strode over to his
horse, unwrapped the bundle behind his saddle and
tossed it to Lou. He nipped the keys and card from her
extended palm. "All right, there it is. This one time
only, don't ask me again. I don't want the other
women or the guys hearing about this, either." He
shook his head and scowled at the two of them. "I
must be crazy. Just remember, *don't ask me again.*"

He was on his horse and moving before they could utter a word. By the time he turned the corner of the barn, the two women were unrolling the pack. They stared down in silence.

"Will you just look at that stuff," Jill said, awed.

"I am," Lou said in deep satisfaction. "I certainly am." She looked up with a grin. "Now that I've *finally* made my goal, do you want a roast beef sandwich?"

Two weeks later, Heather sat at her desk. Once a month, she forced Maude to sit still long enough to hear an accounting of the Oasis expenses. This was the day, and that was what she was supposed to be doing. Instead she was staring out the window watching her pesky guest, Doris, creep up behind Whitey. When she tapped him on the shoulder, he leaped into the air like a startled deer then sagged back against the split-rail fence.

"Have you noticed that the men seem a trifle edgy these days?" Maude asked worriedly, watching Whitey tug his hat over his eyes. "And they're getting thinner, don't you think? I'll have to talk to Barney. Maybe he's working them too hard. Just look at that Whitey, he's losing his belly. Pretty soon, if he closes one eye, he'll look just like a needle."

As Maude clucked over the men's deteriorating condition, Heather arrived at a decision. "Have you noticed that they're the *only* ones who seem to be losing weight?" she asked quietly.

In guilty reflex, Maude dropped her hands to her ample hips. "I've been visiting Bertha too often, I know."

Heather smiled at the doleful admission. "I'm not pointing a finger at you, I'm talking about our clients."

"Clients?" Maude murmured vaguely. "Aren't they having fun?"

Heather's voice was dry. "They're having a whale of a time."

Maude brightened. "Then there's no problem?"

"I guess it all depends on how you look at it." Heather looked away from the window, wincing. Doris, plump and pear-shaped, was stalking a frazzled-looking Whitey. "I never imagined something like this would happen, and I don't know how to handle it."

"Something like what?" Maude took a seat, folded her hands in her lap and gave her attention to Heather.

"Well, for starters, our very first guests discovered Bertha's bakery."

"Oh, dear."

"You can say that again. And they were also driven crazy by Millie's desserts and the meals she cooked for the men." For the first time, she told Maude the entire story, including the tantalizing situation set up by Lou and her friends.

Maude's silver brows knitted together. "Are all of them behaving like that?"

"We're on our third set, with Doris staying on a second week. All of these women know each other and, yes, I think they're calling the next batch and telling them that there are goodies to be found—if they're smart enough to find them. And each new group arrives determined to break the code.''

"It's almost like a scavenger hunt or one of those mystery weekends people go to."

"Almost," Heather agreed dryly.

"And do you think they're finding anything?" Maude's blue eyes were hopeful, but Heather couldn't figure out exactly what she wanted to hear.

"Uh-huh, I think so. Most of them, anyway. All except Doris, and I think that's why she stayed another week."

"Doris isn't . . . very personable, is she?"

"She's a chronic complainer," Heather said flatly. "A pain in the backside, and I think she could be a troublemaker."

The two women stared at each other until Maude finally broke the thoughtful silence. "What do you plan to do?"

Now why wasn't she surprised to hear that? Heather asked herself wryly, knowing she would have been stunned speechless if Maude had offered a solution. "I don't know. I wanted to talk to you before I did anything."

Maude was always willing to talk. She settled deeper in the chair and asked, "What do you consider the worst problems?"

"I see two major ones." Heather propped her elbows on the desk and steepled her fingers. "The first one has a couple of aspects, I think. First, we're not accomplishing our goal, which is to give the woman a refuge from temptation. Second, and even more important from a financial standpoint, our entire business rests on a very shaky foundation, that of the current women not telling the next ones about the bakery. I don't know how long that will last. All it will take is one person."

Maude's brows rose. "Like Doris."

"Exactly."

"And what's the next problem?"

"Your cowboys. These women are either offering bribes for their lunches or driving them crazy with questions, trying to find out where the goodies are stashed."

Maude's grin surprised Heather. "At least it's easy to tell which of the men are giving in to temptation."

"What do you mean?"

"The thin ones are obviously not eating as much as they used to." Maude chuckled fondly. "But just imagine, some of them are riding around in fancy cars they'd never have a chance at normally. That Whitey's probably making out like a bandit."

"You don't mind?"

"What's to mind?" Maude asked with a shrug. "When the men hired on, no one told them that holding out against hungry women was part of their job. If they want to sell their food, go without lunch when they're working out in the fields, that's their choice. I don't mind that part, and I know they'll never tell about the bakery."

"But there are some who are putting up with a lot of aggravation because of their loyalty to you."

Smiling, Maude said, "I'll find some way to reward them. And as for the rest, whatever happens at the end I have a feeling that the men will be talking about this summer for years to come."

Several hours later, sitting on the porch swing, Heather was still thinking about Maude's philosophical attitude. The older woman could afford to be philosophical, she decided. Due to perspicacious ancestors who purchased land when it was cheap and a husband who had turned a small inheritance into a tidy fortune, she wasn't financially dependent upon the success of The Oasis.

Actually, Maude's situation was similar to her own, Heather acknowledged. There was a trust fund established by her grandparents, and the Brandon money was always available if she needed it, but once she'd graduated it had been a point of pride to make it on her own. She was still doing that. So she, too, could survive the demise of The Oasis, but she had an emotional investment in the house, one that she couldn't easily walk away from.

"Heather?" Doris's call was a peremptory demand for attention.

"What on earth happened to you!" Heather hurried down the stairs and put her arm around the portly woman. Doris was flushed from the heat, with perspiration trickling down a face covered with dust. She was also scratched, rumpled and walking with a decided limp. "Are you all right?"

Doris leaned her substantial weight against Heather as she worked her way up the steps. "Do I look all right?" she croaked, falling heavily on the swing. She let out a yelp of anguish as it bucked and skittered beneath her weight. "I've sprained my ankle or broken my leg, or both,'' Glaring out at the yard, corral and barn, she said, "This is a hellish place. I don't know why I came. From the very first day I knew it wasn't the kind of place I'm accustomed to.''

"Then, why did you ask to stay another week?'' Heather kept her voice soothing, reminding herself that the good came with the bad, and if she ever expected to run a bed-and-breakfast she'd have to accept the fact that there would be days—and people— like this.

"Because I'm a glutton for punishment,'' Doris snapped. "And because I...hadn't accomplished something that was important to me.''

Great, Heather thought glumly. If Doris didn't find the bakery this week, she might sign on for a third. For a moment she struggled with the impulse to hand the irksome woman a map, with arrows pointing to Bertha's place.

"And now, here I sit, with a broken leg—or worse. Do you realize that there are holes in the ground out there?''

"Is that what happened, you stepped in a hole?''

"Yes, and when I lost my balance I grabbed for the fence.'' Doris wiggled and the swing protested. "And the fence was so flimsy, it sagged and fell over. It's your obligation to keep things in good repair around here.''

"I thought we did,'' Heather said slowly. "Where were you?''

Doris narrowed her eyes. "Why?''

"So I can make sure that someone repairs the fence. And fills in the hole, of course.''

Not meeting Heather's direct gaze, the older woman mumbled vaguely, "Out there, somewhere." Her broad gesture could have covered half of the ranch. "I got turned around. I don't know where I was half the time." Heaving herself to her feet, she said, "I'm going to my room to clean up. If I can make it."

"Do you want some help?" Heather held her hand out to the lurching woman.

"No. I'm going to be here three more days, so I might as well get used to taking care of myself. But mark my words, if I'm not better by the end of the week you'll be hearing from my lawyer."

"I'll bring you some ice, then help you elevate your leg," Heather told her, heading for the kitchen. A lawsuit, she thought numbly, pulling ice cubes out of the freezer. That's all she needed. Making a mental note to dig out the insurance policy and double-check the liability clause, she wrapped the ice in a towel and headed for Doris's room. When she reached the hall, she stopped. Between coping with a reckless partner, the egos and personalities of the ranch hands, ditto for the clients, and a man who was flat-out trying to drive her crazy, her days had been anything but dull. The cowboys, she reflected wryly, weren't the only ones who would remember this summer for years to come.

Mac found her in the hot tub.

It was late, and the guests had called out their goodnights an hour earlier.

"Hi."

Heather opened one eye. "Hi."

"You look beat."

"Thanks. That's just what I needed to hear."

"Rough day, I take it."

Heather closed her eye. "Doris sprained her ankle this afternoon, and I got to play Florence Nightingale. After catering to her bad-tempered requests all evening, I decided that I'd either slit my wrists or come out here. I didn't think we had a knife sharp enough, so climbing in the hot tub required less effort."

Heather heard the rustle of clothes but was too lazy to investigate. She was not surprised when, a few seconds later, he eased in beside her.

"Poor baby." He slid an arm behind her and lifted her across his lap, pressing her head down until it rested on his shoulder. "Lean on me for a while."

She did exactly that, luxuriating in his easy strength. Heather knew herself well enough to admit that she wasn't a passive woman, one who allowed a man to control a relationship. She was definitely the equal-opportunity type. And for the last six months she had definitely, almost militantly, been the captain of her ship, the officer in charge. But every now and then, she acknowledged, it was a relief to let someone else take the wheel for a while. Someone with strong hands who would steer it on a steady course.

It had been well over six months since she had allowed herself to totally relax in a man's arms, she realized with a sense of surprise. In fact, she couldn't remember the last time. Jerrold had not been the type who offered to take on anyone else's burdens. Looking back on the relationship she had a hard time understanding exactly what the attraction had been. On her side, that was. Jerrold's had been exceedingly obvious at the end.

She gave a gusty sigh and rubbed her cheek against Mac's shoulder, gently kneading the tips of her fingers in the mat of hair on his chest.

"Better now?" His voice rumbled deep in his throat and she smiled, feeling the vibrations against the side of her face.

"Um-hmm."

"Good. I like you like this. Boneless. Melting over me." He touched his thumb to the base of her neck, working down her spine with gentle strokes, stopping low on her back when the fabric of her bathing suit interfered with his explorations. "Soft and fragile," he murmured, "yet strong enough to tie me up in knots." His other hand dropped to her thigh, tracing down to her knee, then following the subtle swell of her calf. "Silky. It should have a poem written about it."

There was a smile in his voice that was as disarming as his touch. Heather snuggled closer and waited to see where his hand would go next.

"Maybe a book," he reflected. "Nah, it would probably be banned."

Book? Heather blinked then sat up with a rush. "Oh, Mac! I forgot to tell you!"

He groaned and his large hands wrapped around her waist, lifted her as if she weighed no more than the fluffy towel at the side of the tub, then settled her firmly on his thighs. "Honey, I love your enthusiasm, but could you send out a warning before you jump around like that?"

"Mac, you were right!" Heather's eyes were round with excitement. "I got a letter from John Melrose today."

"That's good?" He grinned at her animated expression.

"Of course, it is. It's wonderful!"

"Good. Who is he?"

"The editor. The intelligent, perceptive man who wants another article from me. And he's even going to pay me more for the second one!"

"He'd better." Mac pulled her back in his arms and hugged her. Then he set her next to him, leaned over to kiss her on the tip of her nose and said, "I told you it was good."

"It was better than that, it was wonderful," she said modestly.

He grinned. "And so are you."

"Yes, I am." She chuckled. "Simply marvelous."

"Good." His thumb brushed the pulse at the base of her throat. "Because that's the kind of woman I need. When can I have you?"

Heather's smile froze. "For what?" she asked cautiously.

"Forever. To love, to marry, to spend the rest of my life with."

"Oh, Mac," she sighed, brushing her fingers down his cheek, touching his shoulder then dropping her hand to his lap. Her eyes widened and she stiffened, snatching her hand back. "You don't have any clothes on!"

"And you have on too many." He calmly retrieved her hand, dropped a kiss in its palm and put it back where it had been, allowing her to feel the evidence of his need. "Honey, you don't know how much I need you, how much I want to love you."

She gave a shaky laugh. "I'm getting a vague idea."

Mac sighed sharply. "I have to get back to Denver."

Heather felt a sense of loss so acute it stunned her. He had made himself a part of her life. She had grown accustomed to having him near, to sharing the little, everyday things with him, to his sensual teasing, the brush of his big body against hers. And she didn't quite know how she would survive without him.

"Are you ready to say that you'll marry me?"

Her silence was more then enough answer.

"Will you tell me that you love me?"

Heather cleared her throat. "I want you, Mac," she said with painful honesty, "More than I've ever wanted any man, but I don't know if it's love. I once thought I loved someone else and the feeling didn't survive the first hurdle."

"That just proves your intelligence," he told her, dropping a swift kiss on her lips before he stood and stepped up to the porch. "But I need you to do more than want me. I need to be loved." He stepped into his briefs, then pulled on his jeans. "More than anything, I guess I need to know that you trust me to love you and take care of you."

He held out his hand and slowly she grasped it, allowing him to pull her up. Instead of releasing her when she was on her feet he tugged her into his arms, holding her against his bare chest.

His lips brushed hers again and again, until she was dizzy with need. When she was clinging to him, breathless and trembling, he whispered, "In two weeks I'm coming back for my answer."

Chapter Ten

Heather looked up from the telephone on her desk, smiled at the sight of Maude's curly head in the doorway, and waved her in. "Be right with you," she promised, holding the receiver tucked between her ear and shoulder.

On the other end of the line, the telephone was answered in midring. Heather took a deep breath. "Doris? Hi, it's Heather Brandon. I'm just calling to see if your ankle is any better. No? I'm sorry to hear that."

Maude wrinkled her face in a scowl, and Heather grimaced in agreement. "Yes," she said slowly, "we received the letter from your lawyer. Umm, we're sorry it turned out that way, too. We had hoped that The Oasis would provide a relaxing, positive experience for all of our guests. Yes, it *is* too bad."

With a wince, Heather held the receiver and the squawking voice away from her ear. "Yes, I quite understand your position," she replied when the din died down. "There are times when action, unpleasant as it seems, is necessary." She waited again, then, her brows lifting in surprise, Heather repeated, "How am I? Oh, fine. Life is never dull around here." She darted a look at the older woman, who nodded encouragingly. "I've even found time to do some writing. Yes, it's a nice, creative outlet. Who for? Newspapers, mainly."

Heather forged on brightly. "Oh, you'd probably be interested in this, since it's local." She mentioned the name of the largest Phoenix newspaper. "Just this morning, I received a call from the society editor. She's learned that many of the local women have visited The Oasis and asked me to write an article for one of the Sunday editions. What? Oh, what kind?"

Heather looked up and the two women exchanged smiles that had "Gotcha!" written all over them. "Oh, just something chatty and anecdotal," she tossed off in response to the agitated chatter. "You know the type, mentioning some funny or unusual things that have happened. Of course, no name will be mentioned."

She listened politely for a long time. "Well, yes," she finally said. "More than likely I would mention it. After all, it's not every day that a truckful of Indians unload a guest in our front yard. Especially one with brownie crumbs embedded in her shirt, and who is suffering from an obvious overdose of chocolate. As I said, though, no names will be mentioned."

The squawking rose both in register and intensity. Heather held the receiver away from her ear until it died down. "Blackmail?" she asked in astonishment. "Doris, I'm shocked. How could you think such a thing? Besides, I haven't even agreed to do it yet. As I said, I just received the call this morning." Heather smiled, her eyes gleaming with intense satisfaction. "What a pleasant surprise," she purred. "Maude and I have often remarked that you are a most generous and compassionate woman. Yes, it's been nice talking with you, too."

She cradled the receiver and said, "She's calling off the dogs."

"You were wonderful," Maude said warmly. "I didn't know you had it in you."

Grinning, Heather replied, "It all comes from knowing you, dear lady. The experience has added untold depths to my character. I can now lie and blackmail without a blink." She frowned thoughtfully. "But something Doris said did bring up another point."

"What was that?" Maude asked placidly, examining her fingernails with a frown.

"She reminded me that if I wrote such an article, I'd be blowing the whistle on The Oasis. Admitting that there is a bakery nearby."

"She's right," Maude said, scraping at her cuticle.

"I know she is, and I have no intention of writing such a piece, but if *I* could do it, so could anyone else. All it would take is one person to spill the beans."

"I'm surprised that one person wasn't Doris."

"No, she worked too hard finding the bakery. She wasn't going to let anyone else do it the easy way." Heather examined Maude's serene expression. "But, I don't think we can fool ourselves. The Oasis has become a fad. It's known as *the* place to be right now, but none of our guests have left here slimmer than when they arrived. In fact, most of them have gained a pound or two. It can't last much longer. Will you be terribly disappointed?"

Maude's face was like a mirror: it reflected every passing emotion. The only problem was, Heather finally decided, that they passed too quickly and she wasn't adept enough at reading them.

"I've been throwing things," Maude admitted with a sigh.

Heather stared at the other woman. If that cryptic statement was an answer, she needed a deciphering code. "The stress getting to you?" she ventured finally.

"Oh, no." Maude looked surprised. "I find it quite relaxing."

"Um. I guess you can get rid of a lot of tension that way," she agreed blankly. "When do you, uh, throw things most often?" If she could connect the throwing to certain incidents, she mused, she just might be able to—

"Always in the morning, when it's cool."

Heather narrowed her eyes in a speculative gaze while a grin turned up the corners of her mouth. They'd had conversations like this before, and the outcome had *never* been what she'd expected. "Maude—"

"The only problem is that it's hard on the finger-nails."

"I give up." Heather's sudden chuckle seemed to startle Maude. "What are we talking about?"

"Throwing pottery, of course."

Heather blinked. "Are you telling me that you're *making* pottery?"

"Throwing," Maude corrected. "Of course, I am. Isn't that what I said? I met this lady from Taos, and she showed me how. I was hoping to visit her next month—"

"So what you're telling me is that you won't be heartbroken if The Oasis goes out of business?"

Maude shook her head. "Not at all." She grinned. "Besides, some of the men can't afford to lose any more weight. What about you?"

"How will I feel?"

Maude nodded.

"The only part of this operation I enjoyed was fixing up the house," Heather admitted. "I don't like being confined, and I don't want to be responsible for other people."

Maude's sigh was relieved. "Well, that settles that. Now, how can we stop these women from coming?"

Heather stuck a stamp on the last envelope and thumped it energetically with the side of her fist. The exuberant action, unconscious as it was, made her realize exactly how relieved she was. The letters would go in the morning mail, starting the first phase of closing The Oasis for business. She and Maude had agreed that they would return all deposits for dates

falling after the end of the month, with an explana-
tion that The Oasis was once again to be a private
home.

"And will it be?" she had asked curiously, wondering but hesitating to ask precisely what plans
Maude had for the lovely old place.

"There's always Mac's vacations. I think that he'll
have a new appreciation of the house, don't you?"
had been the vague reply.

"He'd better," Heather mumbled to herself,
checking her desk calendar. He'd want to change the
furniture, of course, but she would come back and
haunt him on a weekly basis if he neglected the house.
The least he could do would be to arrange for a cleaner
to come in at regular intervals. And that's exactly what
she would tell him when she saw him. Whenever that
might be.

Two weeks, he had said.

It had been three.

A crisis, he had said when he'd called. At work.

And she believed him. Mac had never been less than
honest with her, even at the beginning when they'd
met. He hadn't tried to conceal his feelings about the
house, nor had he offered her false comfort when
she'd told him about the fiasco with Jerrold. He'd said
bluntly that she was better off without the idiot.
Equally as frankly he'd told her he wasn't after her
money.

He was just as honest about his need and desire. He
didn't play games, and he took risks. He allowed
himself to be vulnerable. That night in the hot tub he

had guided her hand to the hardness of his lower body so she would know the depth of his need, his desire.

Yes, she believed Mac; he was honest to the core. It was too bad that she didn't have the same confidence in herself. She knew she wanted Mac. She *thought* she loved him. Unfortunately she had already proven to herself that her judgment was sadly lacking when it came to men.

Heather stood up, making a small sound of disgust deep in her throat. She had no patience with self-indulgence. If she had any sense, she would forget the most forgettable Jerrold, and concentrate on what destiny had seen fit to gift her with. And she would do exactly that—if the unfortunate experience with her ex-fiancé wasn't still so fresh in her mind. The loss of her trust, her illusions, had hurt far more than the loss of Jerrold.

She turned back to the calendar and marked it, a deeply satisfied smile on her face. Three more weeks and seventeen guests stood between her and freedom.

"Can you believe it, Maude? It's the last week. Two more days, and we're free!"

Heather watched Maude turn on the wheel—which was nothing more than a horizontal, revolving table—and dump an oozing blob of clay on it. Averting her eyes from the mess, she gazed around the workroom at some of Maude's handiwork. She had studied the pieces before and had concluded that either Maude had missed something vital in the instructions, or that she had absolutely no talent. She saw nothing different in the latest lopsided and unsteady creations to alter her opinion.

Picking up a plastic bottle filled with water, Maude liberally sprayed the unsightly mound. She curved her hands around the clay and within seconds gray, gluey slush seeped between her fingers. A look of intense satisfaction crossed her face. "Do you suppose I was forbidden to make mud pies when I was a child?" she wondered aloud. "Yes," she added, proving that she had heard Heather's comment, "we should do something special for our last guests."

"What do you think about a guided tour of Bertha's?" Heather stepped back and wiped a splash of grayish water off her bare leg. To protect her pink shorts and knit top, she moved a stool to a safe distance and perched on it.

"Haven't they found it, yet?"

Heather grinned at Maude's complete lack of concern. "Isn't it odd? We were so uptight about the bakery when we opened, and lately we haven't been able to figure out why it takes the women so long to find it."

"Maybe the men have gotten better at shooing them north."

"Whatever. Speaking of the men, some of them have definitely gotten thinner."

"I always said that this was a perfect place to lose weight." Maude shot a mischievous glance at Heather.

"So you did." The two women giggled, sounding surprisingly alike.

"Have you heard from Mac lately?"

"Umm. Last night."

"And the night before?"

"And the night before that," Heather agreed. "In fact, every night since he left."

"That's a lot of calling. It's been, what? Five weeks?"

"That's right." Heather eyed the rotating mound with interest. "What's this one going to be?"

Maude looked up in surprise. "I don't know. I wait for it to tell me."

Which could be part of the problem with the originals that lined the walls, Heather mused. They obviously hadn't spoken up quickly enough.

Maude coughed delicately. "About Mac."

"Umm?"

"I thought he'd be back before this."

"He intended to be, but several problems have come up at the paper and he's needed to be there." Plus the fact that he seemed unusually adept at taking her emotional temperature over the telephone, and she had a strong feeling that he wouldn't be back until he knew he'd get the answer he wanted.

"You're satisfied with the arrangement?"

Heather nodded serenely. "For now."

Tilting her head, Maude took a long look at her young friend. Too long as it turned out, because a section of the unattended clay shot up like a geyser. Heather's fascinated stare and her pointing finger turned Maude's attention back to the wheel.

"Well!" Maude beamed. "Will you look at that! It's a vase. What did I tell you?" She futilely poked at the wavering column as it circled, denting one side. "This will be one of my keepers."

While Heather sat transfixed, watching her friend's attempt to control the masterpiece, warm hands closed around her waist, lifted and turned her against a hard, substantial body.

"Mac!"

"'Bout time," Maude said, ducking when the long neck of the vase whipped around, growing another two inches.

Mac's palms framed Heather's face, turning it up to his. "My God, I've missed you." His green eyes locked with hers, a flash of intense hunger gleaming in their depths, taking her breath away. Then his head lowered and his mouth moved across hers, tasting, testing in fleeting forays before settling on the soft, inviting warmth of her lips.

"Drat! I'm losing control."

At the sound of Maude's voice, Mac lifted his head, tightening his arms and keeping Heather right where she was. He looked over her shoulder, staring at an object that resembled a gray cobra, spinning in circles, bobbing and weaving as it came out of a basket.

"What the hell *is* that thing?"

The blank astonishment in his voice, coming on the heels of the overwhelming sensuality of his kiss, was Heather's undoing. She rubbed her cheek against his chest, and tried to control the tremors running through her. "A vase," she choked in a watery voice.

"The hell you say."

"Watch out," Maude warned. "I'm going to lose it." She turned off the wheel and watched mournfully as her magnum opus collapsed into a heap that looked like an elephant on its stomach, trunk stretched out

before it. Sighing philosophically, she scraped up the
clay and dumped it in a container and closed the lid.

She tilted her cheek for Mac's kiss. Taking Heather
with him, he moved closer and leaned down to touch
her cheek with his lips.

"I've been hard at work while you've been lolly-
gagging in the city," Maude boasted. She waved an
arm at the shelves filled with her handiwork. "See?"

Mac surveyed the conglomeration of atrocities and
shuddered. Fortunately they were interrupted before
he could comment.

Barney knocked on the open door. "Heather?
There's a fella outside who wants to see you."

Looking up from where she was washing her hands
at the sink, Maude said, "Why didn't you invite him
in?"

"Because he said he'd rather poke around outside."

A tingle of warning worked its way down Heather's spine. She only knew one person—one man—who
would ask for her, then stay outside to examine property. Her brother. A man who habitually bought
beautiful sites outside of towns and promptly plunked
buildings and shopping malls on them.

"Maude," she ordered briskly, "whatever you do,
don't listen to a word he says." When she turned to
leave, Mac was right beside her. By the time they
reached the porch, he was not only beside her, he had
his hand resting on her hip and a very proprietary
gleam in his eyes.

"Les!" Heather broke loose, trotted down the stairs
and launched herself at the waiting man. He was big

and quick. He caught Heather and whirled her around. By the time he set her on her feet, checked her over, hugged and kissed her, Mac was waiting.

Now that he was closer, he could see that the man had Heather's brown eyes. In fact, he was a taller, broader, tougher, masculine version of Heather. He was also staring at Mac with a hint of challenge in his dark eyes. What the hell, Mac decided, might as well get this show on the road.

He reached out for Heather and drew her back against him, tucking her under his arm. He shoved back his hat and returned the stare. "You the brother?" he drawled.

Les nodded, one dark brow arching.

"I'm the fiancé."

"Mac!"

Both men looked at her flushed face, both waiting politely. When she simply gazed back, looking from one to the other in amazement, they resumed staring at each other, neither one giving an inch.

"I haven't heard that from her yet," Les said, nodding in Heather's direction.

"You will."

Not a bit happy with the way things were going, Heather jumped into the fray. "Maude," she said, reaching out and tugging the older woman closer, "I'd like you to meet my brother, Les. Les, my partner, Maude Gunther. And this is Wade Mackenzie."

Les's smile charmed Maude. So did all of the proper things he said to her. When Les turned back to her nephew, he wasn't smiling.

Mac slid his hands in the back pockets of his jeans. "My friends and family call me Mac," he said blandly.

Les didn't hesitate. "How do you do?"

Heather rolled her eyes, then burst into speech. "This is a surprise," she said chattily to her brother. "I thought you had dropped off the face of the earth."

"I just got back from another trip to California and decided to swing by here on the way home." He slid a level look at Mac. "None too soon, it seems."

Sighing, Heather tried again. Grabbing her brother's arm, she swung him around to face the valley. "What do you think of our front yard?" she asked, a sudden rush of love for the harsh land softening her voice.

Les, however, was made of sterner stuff. He turned to Maude. "Do you know what a gold mine you're sitting on? My God, I could build a whole city out there."

"Philistine!" Heather laughed up at him. "Barbarian! Maude, I told you, don't listen to a thing he says. This smooth-tongued sharpie will buy your land and have buildings sprouting up like carrots before you even know what's happening."

After his assessing gaze swept the area, Les murmured absently, "Of course, you'd have to raze the buildings."

"Over my dead body," Heather said spiritedly. She looked at Mac and Maude, enjoying the amused indulgence in their eyes. "Can you believe we grew up in the same family, sharing the same genes? Everything I fight to preserve, he wants to squash with bulldozers.''

Les turned to her. "No," he said slowly, taking in the muscular arm around her shoulders, "some things I try to protect."

"Sometimes," Mac said to no one in particular, "people need freedom more than they need safeguarding."

Les ignored him. "What are you going to do now that you've decided to close your business?" he asked Heather.

Well, hell, Mac thought. He had wanted the ball rolling, but not quite this fast. Wondering how his cagey lady would react, he said, "She's got several options, as I see it." Heather closed her mouth and glared at him. "First, she's moving to Denver."

Les turned to her, one brow shooting up. "You are?"

Heather stared at Mac, her narrow-eyed gaze warning him. "I am?" she asked calmly.

"You are," he assured her without shifting his gaze from her brother's face. "Then, your options open up. I've found at least thirty old homes in the area that need your brand of TLC. There are probably a lot more. Those are just to start with. You can redecorate and convert to your heart's content. Or if you want to try your wings, you can buy one, renovate it, use it for office space and hold seminars to train others how to do the same thing. Then there's always your writing. You can keep on doing articles, try your hand at a monthly newsletter or even start a magazine."

"Is that it?" she asked. "Anything else?"

"Yeah. Before you do any of that, you marry me."

"I do?" She tapped her foot in a warning that he completely ignored.

"Yep." He ran his thumb down her cheek in a gentle caress.

And at that moment, Heather realized that he understood her better than she understood herself. He was right, she decided, a smile lifting the corners of her mouth. She *was* going to marry him, and damn his eyes, he *knew* it! As far as that went, he knew too much for her own good. He had driven her crazy with telephone calls so sexy that they had probably singed the wires between Denver and Phoenix, waited for *five weeks*, all because he had known she needed the time, the reassurance. And now, today, he had come to claim her, knowing just as surely that she was ready.

She sighed. Noisily. Letting him see her exasperation. He just smiled. Again. It was going to be difficult keeping one step ahead of this untamed, unpredictable half cowboy, half editor, she reflected, but damn, was she going to have fun trying!

Les's voice prodded her. "Do you?" he asked. When she blinked questioningly, he added roughly, "Marry him?"

She looked at Mac, her smile blinding. "Yes."

He caught his breath. "When?"

She found that she was having trouble breathing, too. The combination of love and hunger in his eyes was making her dizzy. "As soon as possible," she whispered.

Mac touched her face with a shaky hand. He was no longer teasing. "We'll fly to Vegas this afternoon. If you want, we'll do it all over when your folks are back and we can get both families together."

Les cleared his throat. Once he had Heather's attention, he said, "Are you interested in hearing what I know about him?"

Her reply came fast; it was very clear and direct. "No. I've learned everything I need to know about Mac. What I don't know, I want the pleasure of discovering myself."

Les shrugged, satisfied. "If it makes any difference, his family has almost as much money as ours."

"More," Mac corrected blandly.

The two men grinned.

"I do so love a happy ending," Maude sighed. Then she latched on to Les's arm and said briskly, "Let's give the lovebirds some time to themselves. Come inside and have some lemonade, and I'll show you my workroom."

Mac lifted his wife and carried her from the round, rumpled bed to the pink-and-red heart-shaped spa. He slipped into the pulsing hot water and turned Heather to face him, sighing with satisfaction when she wrapped her arms around his neck and relaxed against him. Her soft breasts pressed against his chest and her knees eased down the sides of his thighs. It was an arrangement designed to drive a man wild, he mused contentedly.

Heather murmured, "Thank you, darling."

Tightening his arm, he asked, "For what?"

She opened her eyes and looked around the bridal suite. "For bringing me to such a deliciously decadent room."

"I didn't exactly plan it," he said wryly. "It was the only room they had left."

"It's unbelievably tacky," she told him with an approving smile.

He sighed. "It falls in line with everything else we've done. All in all, it's been a hell of a courtship."

She reared back, ignoring his wince. "You've been courting me?"

"Of course." He was indignant. "Couldn't you tell?"

"You were the most provoking man I'd ever met."

"You needed stirring up."

"And you left me alone for *five weeks*."

His hands slid down to her bottom, kneading gently. "You needed the time."

"You never tried to make love to me." Silky lashes half concealed her questioning glances.

Brushing his fingers up her waist and over her rib cage to the satiny underside of her breasts, he said softly, "I made love to you with every word I spoke and every breath I took."

Heather inhaled sharply. "You never tried to get me in bed," she amended.

Mac gave a hard laugh that indicated the depths of his frustration. "Where?" he demanded. "You wouldn't leave the ranch. I couldn't take you to Maude's, and women were tumbling out the windows at your place. The ranch hands were everywhere else."

Dropping a kiss on his chin, Heather smiled. "Sounds like you considered all the options."

"You bet."

She snuggled closer. "Were you surprised when Maude gave us the house for a wedding present?"

"Grateful. I was afraid she was going to hand us some of those atrocities in her workroom."

Heather giggled. "They'll probably come along later."

"Oh, God."

"Don't worry, I'll fill them full of dried flowers." After a moment, she sighed. "I suppose you'll want everything back the way it was."

"We can keep the hot tub," he said promptly.

"What about the rest?"

"Toss out the Exercycles, get a king-size bed and bring back those big chairs and couches. You can have them re-covered," he offered generously.

Heather pictured the two of them curled up on the massive couch and decided that all was not lost. She felt Mac move convulsively beneath her and smiled. Indeed, all was not lost.

"Very impressive," she lauded, shifting her weight until he groaned and tightened his arms. "I was afraid that you'd never—"

His mouth stopped her teasing. When he lifted his head, the hunger in his eyes stunned her.

She touched his face. "Mac?"

"I'll always be able to love you." His thumbs grazed her nipples and she gave a delicious gasp.

She sighed. "Oh, Mac."

His hands cupped around the resilient flesh of her bottom, urging her hips closer to his.

"Ahhh."

"I love you, Heather."

"What are you—"

"Today."

"Here?"

"Tomorrow."

"Oh!"

"Always."

"*Mac!*"

* * * * *

COMING NEXT MONTH

#712 HARVEY'S MISSING—Peggy Webb
A Diamond Jubilee Title!
Janet Hall was in search of her missing weekend dog, Harvey, but what she found was Dan Albany, who claimed Harvey was *his* week*day* dog. Would the two ever agree on anything?

#713 JUST YOU AND ME—Rena McKay
The Loch Ness monster was less elusive than the blue-eyed MacNorris men of Norbrae Castle. Vacationing Lynn Marquet was falling fast for Mike MacNorris, one of the mystifying Scottish clansmen...or was she?

#714 MONTANA HEAT—Dorsey Kelley
Nanny Tracy Wilborough expected to find peace of mind in Montana. What she hadn't counted on was exciting rodeo performer Nick Roberts lassoing her heart!

#715 A WOMAN'S TOUCH—Brenda Trent
When Troy Mayhan first met neighbor Shelly Hall, they literally fell into each other's arms. Now the sexy ex-football player was determined to have her fall again—in love with him!

#716 JUST NEIGHBORS—Marcine Smith
Loner Wyatt Neville had never had a sweet tooth—or been tempted to indulge in romance—until delectable Angela Cowan moved her cookie factory next door to his home....

#717 HIS BRIDE TO BE—Lisa Jackson
The contract said she was his bride to be for two weeks only. But two weeks was all it took for Hale Donovan to know that Valerie Pryce was his love for a lifetime.

AVAILABLE THIS MONTH:

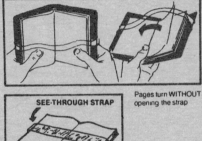

Silhouette Special Edition®

proudly presents

Taming Natasha
by
NORA ROBERTS

Once again, award-winning author Nora Roberts weaves her special brand of magic this month in TAMING NATASHA (SSE #583). Toy shop owner Natasha Stanislaski is a pussycat with Spence Kimball's little girl, but to Spence himself she's as ornery as a caged tiger. Will some cautious loving sheath her claws and free her heart from captivity?

TAMING NATASHA, by Nora Roberts, has been selected to receive a special laurel—the Award of Excellence. This month look for the distinctive emblem on the cover. It lets you know there's something truly special inside.

Available now

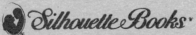